THOMAS DEGAN

The Harmonic Divide

Book 1

First edition

ISBN: 979-8-9944730-0-9

This book was professionally typeset on Reedsy.
Find out more at reedsy.com

1

The Sky Remembers

The wind found her before the sun did.

Aiyana stood on the launching ledge of Wakana Station, three thousand feet above the valley floor, and felt the air move against her like something alive. It came from the west, carrying the cold green scent of pine forests and snowmelt, and it wrapped around her sky-suit with the gentle insistence of a current testing a stone. She closed her eyes. Let her breathing slow. The suit's membrane responded to each exhale, tightening across her shoulders, loosening at her ribs, a second skin learning the rhythm of her body.

Above her, Sitala circled.

The golden eagle rode the thermals in wide, patient arcs, her wingspan catching the first amber light cresting the Cascadia peaks. Through the bond, Aiyana felt what Sitala felt: the texture of the wind at altitude, the subtle pressure differentials that meant lift or drag, the deep animal satisfaction of flight. It was not thought, exactly. Not language. It was older than that, a knowing that lived in the blood and bone, in the place where breath became motion.

Today was the day. After three years of training, four failed attempts, and one spectacular crash that had left her with a scar along her left forearm, Aiyana Waketah would complete her initiation flight. She would earn her place among the Harmonic Engineers of the Many Nations Alliance. She would become what her father had been, and his mother before him, and her brother,

She stopped the thought there. Pressed it down into the quiet space below her lungs where she kept the things she couldn't afford to feel. Not today.

"Your heart rate is climbing."

Elder Nayeli Cross-the-River stood behind her, a slight woman with iron-gray braids and the kind of stillness that made nervous students more nervous. She had been Aiyana's mentor for two years. She had also been her father's mentor, decades ago, a fact she rarely mentioned and Aiyana rarely forgot.

"I know," Aiyana said. "I'm working on it."

"The suit knows too. It will compensate, but compensation is not harmony. You cannot fight the air and expect it to carry you."

"I'm not fighting."

"You are. I can see it in your shoulders." Nayeli moved to stand beside her at the ledge's edge. The old woman showed no fear of the drop, she had been flying longer than Aiyana had been alive. "You are thinking of all the ways you might fail. Stop. The sky does not care about your fears. It only cares about your presence."

Aiyana opened her eyes. The valley spread below them like a living map: the silver thread of the Wakana River cutting through forests that had never known clear-cutting, the distant gleam of the capital's bio-luminescent towers, the Wind Spine array marching east along the ridge like vertebrae made of light and living wood. This was her home. This was what she had trained to protect.

"What if I'm not ready?" The words came out smaller than she intended.

Nayeli was quiet for a long moment. When she spoke, her voice had lost its teaching edge. "When your father stood on this ledge for his initiation, he asked me the same question. Do you know what I told him?"

"What?"

"That readiness is a story we tell ourselves to avoid the terror of beginning. The truth is simpler: you step off the ledge, or you don't. The sky will teach you the rest." She placed a weathered hand on Aiyana's shoulder. "Your father stepped. So did your brother. So will you."

The mention of Kele sent a pulse of something through her chest, not quite pain, not quite longing. Something in between. She pushed it down again. Later. She would feel it later.

"The flight path," Nayeli continued, her tone returning to instruction. "Recite it."

Aiyana straightened. This, at least, she knew. "North along the ridge to Wind Spine Tower Seven. Hold position at the primary resonance point for sixty seconds to demonstrate harmonic calibration. Then east through the Needle Pass, altitude no higher than four thousand feet to test low-current navigation. South along the river back to Wakana. Total distance: forty-three kilometers. Target time: under two hours."

"And if you encounter turbulence in the Pass?"

"Ascend to find cleaner air, even if it means exceeding the

altitude ceiling. The ceiling is a guideline, not a death wish."

"And if your suit loses harmonic sync?"

"Land immediately. Find root contact. Wait for recalibration. The suit cannot fly without the Bioweb, and I cannot fly without the suit."

Nayeli nodded, something like approval flickering in her dark eyes. "You have learned the words. Now forget them. Let your body remember what your mind knows." She stepped back from the ledge. "Sitala is waiting. So is the sky. Do not keep them waiting longer."

Aiyana turned back to the open air. The sun had crested the peaks now, flooding the valley with gold and rose. Sitala cried out once, a sound that meant

ready, that meant *come*, that meant *fly with me*.

She stepped off the ledge.

* * *

The fall lasted two seconds, maybe three. Long enough for gravity to claim her, for the wind to scream past her ears, for the ancient lizard part of her brain to shriek that she had made a terrible mistake.

Then the suit woke up.

It was not a mechanical activation, nothing clicked or whirred or powered on. The membrane simply remembered what it was for. It had been grown from living fibers, cultivated in the great Weaving Houses of the southern nations, infused with the same bio-resonant compounds that let the Bioweb carry information across a continent. When Aiyana fell, the suit felt her falling. When she spread her arms, it spread with her, catching the wind in surfaces that shifted and adapted faster than any manufactured wing could dream of.

She leveled out fifty feet above the tree line, her heart

hammering, her breath ragged with exhilaration. Above her, Sitala banked and dove, matching her altitude, and through the bond Aiyana felt the eagle's fierce joy,

yes, yes, finally, fly with me, fly,

They flew north along the ridge.

The Wind Spine towers rose ahead of her, spaced at precise intervals along the mountain's spine. Each tower was a hundred feet tall, grown from living wood that had been shaped over decades into spiraling columns of impossible grace. They were conduits, not generators, they captured the wind's kinetic energy, translated it into harmonic resonance, and fed that resonance into the Bioweb network that connected every city, every station, every living thing in the Alliance. Aiyana had studied their design for three years. She had memorized their frequencies, analyzed their failure modes, learned to read their health the way a physician reads a pulse.

But she had never flown through them before. Not like this. Not as an engineer.

As she approached Tower Seven, the easternmost installation, closest to the Frontier and the gray territories beyond, she felt the harmonic field before she saw it. It was a vibration in her chest, a subsonic hum that made her teeth ache and her bones sing. The suit responded automatically, adjusting its membrane to resonate with the tower's frequency, and suddenly Aiyana was not just flying through the air. She was flying through

sound. She was part of the music the tower made with the wind.

She held position at the resonance point, counting seconds, letting the harmonic wash over her. Through the Bioweb connection, she could feel the data flowing beneath her, not as numbers or code, but as something more organic. Conversations in distant cities. The slow pulse of forest growth monitored by agricultural stations. Weather patterns tracked by sky-watchers on the coast. All of it moving through the network like blood through veins, like breath through lungs.

Sixty seconds. She tilted east toward the Needle Pass.

The Pass was narrow, carved between two granite peaks that funneled wind into unpredictable currents. Aiyana dropped her altitude as instructed, skimming below the four-thousand-foot ceiling, and immediately felt the air turn treacherous. Crosswinds battered her from the left. Downdrafts tried to slam her into the rock. The suit compensated, adapted, but it could only do so much, the rest was her, her instincts, her willingness to move

with the chaos rather than against it.

Sitala stayed above the turbulence, circling, watching. Through the bond, Aiyana felt the eagle's attention, not worried, exactly, but vigilant. Ready to dive if needed. Ready to guide her out.

She didn't need the help. She found the rhythm of the Pass, the way the currents cycled, the brief windows of calm between gusts, and she threaded through them like water through stones. By the time she emerged on the southern side, her arms were burning and her lungs were heaving, but she was grinning so hard her cheeks hurt.

The river glittered below her. Wakana Station gleamed in the distance. She had done it.

She followed the water home.

* * *

The ceremony was small, as all engineering ceremonies were. A dozen people gathered in the Wakana Hall, Nayeli, the station administrators, and a handful of other engineers who had taken time from their work to witness. And her mother.

Takoda Waketah stood near the back of the hall, her silver-streaked hair bound in the traditional style of the coastal nations where she had been born. She was watching Aiyana with an expression that was proud and sad and distant all at once, the expression she had worn, Aiyana realized, for the past five years. Since Aiyana's father had died in the Tower Three incident. Since Kele had left for the Frontier.

Nayeli spoke the formal words. Aiyana recited the engineer's oath, to maintain, to protect, to serve the balance between technology and world. A sigil was pressed into the collar of her suit, marking her as certified, qualified, responsible. There was applause. There were handshakes. Someone had brought honey cakes from the valley bakery, and they were very good.

But the whole time, Aiyana kept looking toward the door. Kept waiting for it to open. Kept expecting to see a tall figure with their father's eyes and their mother's stubborn jaw, grinning that reckless grin and saying

I told you I'd make it back, little bird.

The door stayed closed.

After the ceremony, her mother found her on the observation deck overlooking the valley. The sun was setting now, painting the sky in shades of copper and wine. Sitala had settled on a perch nearby, preening her feathers with the self-satisfied air of an eagle who had flown very well today and knew it.

"Your father would be proud," Takoda said. She said this at least once a week. It never stopped hurting.

"I know."

"Kele too."

Aiyana turned to look at her mother. "Have you heard from

him?"

The pause was answer enough. Takoda's hands moved to the railing, gripping it as if the deck might pitch beneath her. "Not in three months. But the Frontier communications are always unreliable. You know that."

"Three months is a long time."

"He's doing important work."

"Is he?" The words came out sharper than Aiyana intended. "Or is he doing work that makes him feel important while the rest of us wonder if he's alive?"

Takoda flinched. It was a small movement, quickly controlled, but Aiyana saw it. And felt, immediately, the familiar guilt that always followed when she let her frustration with Kele escape.

"I'm sorry," she said. "I didn't mean, "

"You meant it." Takoda's voice was gentle. "And you're not wrong to feel it. Your brother made a choice that hurt us. He believed he was doing the right thing. Those two truths don't cancel each other out."

The memory surfaced before Aiyana could stop it: the last real conversation she'd had with Kele, three days before he left for the Frontier.

They had stood on the observation deck of their family's home, much as she stood with her mother now. Kele had already packed. Had already made his decision. He was telling her, not asking.

"Someone has to try," he'd said. *"We can't just keep watching them decay from a distance, pretending their collapse won't eventually touch us."*

"Bridge-building is naive," she'd shot back. *"They don't want bridges. They want what we have, and they'll take it if we give*

them the chance."

"You sound like the border hawks. Like the people who think isolation is the same as safety." His voice had been patient, which somehow made it worse. *"I'm not asking you to agree with me, Aiyana. I'm asking you to understand that I have to try."*

"And if you die trying? If you disappear into the gray lands and we never know what happened?"

He had looked at her with their father's eyes, and for a moment she'd seen something that might have been doubt. Then it was gone, replaced by the certainty that had always been his greatest strength and his greatest flaw.

"Then at least I'll have tried."

She hadn't said goodbye when he left. Hadn't even watched him go. She'd told herself it was anger. Now, standing beside her mother with the same stars overhead, she knew it had been fear. Fear that if she watched him walk away, she'd have to admit she might never see him walk back.

They stood in silence for a while, watching the light fade. Somewhere below, in the valley's evening shadow, a wolf pack began to sing, the long, haunting notes that meant safety and territory and

we are here, we are here. Aiyana wondered if Kele could hear wolves where he was. She wondered if he thought of home when he did.

"Elder Nayeli told me something today," Takoda said. "Before the ceremony."

"What?"

"There's a diplomatic summit in two weeks. At Threshold, on the Frontier. The first formal negotiation with the Pale Cities in fifteen years." Takoda's expression was careful, controlled. "They need technical advisors. Engineers who can speak to

Wind Spine operations, Bioweb protocols. Nayeli recommended you."

Aiyana stared at her. "I just finished my initiation today. I'm the most junior engineer at the station."

"You're also one of the most talented. Nayeli's words, not mine." A small smile. "Though I happen to agree."

"The Frontier." Aiyana turned the word over in her mind. The Frontier, where her brother had gone. The Frontier, where the world their ancestors had built gave way to ruins and ash and the gray lands beyond. "Why would the council send me?"

"Because you're young enough to have no history with the Pale Cities. No grievances. No preconceptions." Takoda paused. "And because Chogan Grayfeather asked for you specifically."

The name landed like a stone in still water. Chogan Grayfeather, the Alliance's senior diplomat, the architect of the last three decades of uneasy peace, the man who had been trying to prevent war with the Pale Cities since before Aiyana was born. He was a legend. He was also, she remembered, one of the few people who had publicly supported Kele's decision to work on the Frontier.

"Why would he ask for me?"

"I don't know." Takoda reached out and brushed a strand of hair from Aiyana's face, a gesture from childhood, from a time when the world had been smaller and safer. "But I think you should go. I think you need to go."

"Because of Kele?"

"Because of you. Because you've spent five years training to protect something, and now you need to understand what you're protecting it from. The Pale Cities aren't just stories, Aiyana. They're real people who made different choices than we did. You can't defend our way of life if you don't understand theirs."

Aiyana thought of the initiation flight. The Wind Spine towers rising from the ridge. The Bioweb humming beneath her like a living thing. All of it was so beautiful, so right, so obviously the way things should be. How could anyone choose differently? How could anyone look at what the Alliance had built and decide they wanted something else?

But her brother had looked east, and he had gone.

"I'll go," she said. "Tell Nayeli I'll go."

Takoda nodded, unsurprised. Perhaps she had known what Aiyana would choose before Aiyana did. Mothers were like that, sometimes.

They embraced briefly, and then Takoda left to find Nayeli. Aiyana stayed on the observation deck, watching the darkness deepen over the valley. The stars were coming out now, real stars, not the artificial lights of the Pale Cities that she had seen in images, the false constellations that burned all night and blotted out the sky.

Sitala stirred on her perch, ruffling her feathers. Through the bond, Aiyana felt a question, not in words, but in sensation. Something like:

Restless. Why?

Aiyana walked over and ran her fingers along the eagle's back, feeling the warmth of her, the steady pulse of her heart. "I don't know yet," she murmured. "But I think we're going to find out."

She looked east, toward the Frontier, toward the gray lands, toward whatever was waiting for her in the place where two worlds met and neither one trusted the other. Somewhere out there, her brother was doing work she didn't understand. Somewhere out there, an enemy she had never met was preparing to sit across a table from her people and pretend to negotiate peace.

Somewhere out there, the sky was different. Pale and strange and full of smoke.

She wondered what it felt like to fly through air that had forgotten how to sing.

She wondered if she would ever find out.

2

The Weight of Gray

The light in Nova-Providence was always the same.

Elias Harren had never thought about this before. It was simply the way things were: the atmospheric processors hummed on the city's outer ring, filtering the air and calibrating the sky's brightness to optimal productivity levels. Morning light at six hundred lumens, gradually increasing to the nine-hundred-lumen peak of midday, then tapering toward the soft amber of evening. Consistent. Predictable. Safe.

He stood at the window of his small apartment on the forty-third floor of Residential Block Eleven, watching the city wake beneath him. The towers of Nova-Providence rose in ordered ranks, steel and glass catching the manufactured dawn, their surfaces alive with the scroll of Signal Mesh broadcasts. News. Productivity reports. Public service announcements. The usual morning rhythm.

Citizens of the Pale Cities, your contributions matter. Today's industrial output target: 97.3%. Together, we build tomorrow.

The words drifted past his awareness, unanchored and unheld. He had grown up with the Mesh; it was simply the texture

13

of the world, no more remarkable than the hum of ventilation or the distant rumble of transit lines. He finished his morning tea, checked his reflection in the mirror, and decided he looked presentable enough for the Cultural Ministry.

Today was going to be a good day. He could feel it.

* * *

The Ministry of Cultural Preservation occupied floors sixty through seventy-five of the Doctrine Tower, a massive spire in the administrative quarter that had been built, according to official history, on the site of the first colonial settlement. Elias had worked there for two years, ever since completing his certification at the Academy of Historical Sciences. It was a good posting. Respectable. His mother had cried when he received the appointment.

He took the express lift to the sixty-eighth floor, where the Cultural Documentation division maintained its offices. The corridors were clean, well-lit, lined with display cases showing artifacts from the Founding Era. Elias passed them every day, but he still found himself pausing occasionally to look: the original charter of the First Assembly, preserved under glass. A tattered flag from the Long March, when the ancestors had fled the western territories. A reproduction of the Declaration of Separation, the document that had formalized the Pale Cities' independence from the chaos of the ungoverned lands.

These were the touchstones of his people's story. The proof that they had survived, had built, had
endured. Every child in Nova-Providence learned this history. Elias had always found comfort in it.

"Harren. My office."

Director Marsh's voice cut through his reverie. Elias turned to find his superior standing in the doorway of the corner office, a thin man with thinning hair and the perpetually harried expression of someone who believed himself underappreciated. Which, in fairness, he probably was. The Cultural Documentation division was not a prestigious posting. It was where the Ministry sent people who were competent but uninspired, reliable but unremarkable.

Elias had always assumed he would spend his career here, slowly rising through the ranks until he became another Director Marsh, harried and underappreciated in his turn. It was not an exciting future, but it was a stable one. In the Pale Cities, stability was its own kind of success.

He followed Marsh into the office. The director closed the door behind them, a gesture that made Elias's stomach tighten. Closed-door meetings usually meant problems.

"Sit," Marsh said, gesturing to a chair. He moved behind his desk and began shuffling papers, a nervous habit that Elias had learned to read as either very good or very bad news. "I've received a directive from the Council. Regarding the Threshold Summit."

Elias sat straighter. Everyone knew about the summit. It had been all over the Mesh for weeks: the first formal diplomatic engagement with the Many Nations Alliance in fifteen years. A chance, the broadcasts said, to demonstrate the Pale Cities' commitment to peaceful coexistence while firmly establishing boundaries and expectations. Elias had followed the coverage with more interest than most of his colleagues. The MNA fascinated him. Always had.

"The delegation requires a cultural attaché," Marsh continued. "Someone to document the proceedings, observe MNA social practices, contribute to our understanding of their... methods." He said the last word with a slight curl of distaste, as if the MNA's methods were something faintly unsanitary. "Your name was submitted for consideration."

Elias blinked. "My name?"

"You have a background in comparative cultural studies. Your thesis on MNA agricultural symbolism was noted." Marsh's tone suggested he found this fact mildly baffling. "The Doctrine Office believes you may have... insights."

"I would be part of the official delegation?"

"Junior attaché. You would report to Chief Doctrine Keeper Drax directly." Marsh leaned back in his chair, and for a moment his expression shifted from harried to something almost like envy. "This is an opportunity, Harren. The kind that doesn't come twice. I trust you understand what's being offered."

Elias understood. He understood that junior attachés who performed well at high-profile events did not remain junior for long. He understood that the Doctrine Office's interest in him meant someone powerful had noticed his work, had seen potential where Director Marsh saw only another reliable cog in the Ministry's machinery. He understood that his mother would cry again, this time with joy.

"When do I leave?" he asked.

"Three days. You'll receive a full briefing from Keeper Drax's office tomorrow. Until then, review everything we have on MNA diplomatic protocols. And Harren?" Marsh's eyes met his, and for a moment the harried administrator was gone, replaced by something sharper. "Remember what you're representing. The Pale Cities don't send observers to learn from the MNA. We send them to

understand the MNA. There's a difference."

Elias nodded, though he wasn't entirely sure he grasped the

distinction. Wasn't understanding a form of learning? Wasn't learning the whole point of sending observers in the first place?

But these were questions for later. For now, there was only the bright, impossible fact of what had just happened: Elias Harren, junior cultural documentarian, was going to see the Many Nations Alliance with his own eyes. He was going to stand in the same room as the people his textbooks had described as primitives clinging to obsolete ways. He was going to find out if any of it was true.

He left Director Marsh's office feeling like he was walking on air. The Mesh screens in the corridor were cycling through their usual broadcasts, but Elias barely noticed. His mind was already racing ahead, imagining what he would see, what he would learn, what he would write in his reports.

Citizens, remember: curiosity is valuable. Loyalty is essential.

The words scrolled past, and Elias felt them settle into him like an old friend's advice. Curiosity and loyalty. That was exactly what he intended to bring.

* * *

His mother lived in the eastern residential district, in a small apartment that had once housed his entire family: his father, his mother, himself, and his younger sister, Calla, who had died of respiratory fever when Elias was twelve. The apartment felt emptier now. Too many rooms for one person. But Vera Harren had refused all suggestions that she relocate to something smaller.

"This is where I raised my children," she always said. "This is where I'll stay until they carry me out."

Elias found her in the kitchen, preparing the evening meal. The apartment smelled of reconstituted vegetables and synthetic protein, the standard fare of the middle residential tiers.

Vera looked up when he entered, and her face immediately shifted into the expression of cautious hope that Elias had come to recognize as her default response to his visits.

"You're early," she said. "Is everything alright?"

"Everything's fine." He crossed the kitchen and kissed her cheek, feeling the papery softness of her skin. She was getting older. He tried not to notice, but it was becoming harder to ignore. "Better than fine, actually. I have news."

He told her about the summit, about the delegation, about the opportunity that had fallen into his lap like a gift from the city itself. Vera listened with her hands pressed together, her eyes growing wider with each detail. When he finished, she sat down heavily in one of the kitchen chairs.

"The Frontier," she said. "They're sending you to the Frontier."

"Not the Frontier exactly. Threshold. It's a neutral site, technically outside both territories."

"But you'll have to travel through the Frontier to get there." Her voice had gone flat, the excitement draining out of it. "Through the dead zones. Past the boundary markers."

"Mother, the delegation will have full security. Captain Lucian Ford is commanding the escort personally. Nothing is going to happen."

"Your father said the same thing." The words came out quiet, almost involuntary. Vera's hands twisted in her lap. "Before his survey mission. He said the boundary zones were perfectly safe, that the MNA wouldn't interfere with a scientific expedition, that I was worrying over nothing."

Elias felt the familiar weight settle into his chest. His father had died when Elias was sixteen, part of a geological survey team that had ventured too far into contested territory.

The official report said equipment failure. Elias had always suspected there was more to it, but the details had been classified under Frontier Security protocols. He had learned, over the years, not to ask questions that wouldn't be answered.

"This is different," he said gently. "This is a diplomatic mission. Both sides have agreed to safe passage. The MNA wants this summit to happen as much as we do."

"Do they?" Vera looked up at him, and there was something in her eyes that Elias rarely saw: not fear, exactly, but a kind of weary skepticism. "The MNA doesn't think the way we do, Elias. Their whole society is built on... on communion with the land, on traditions we abandoned centuries ago. They look at our cities and see a disease. They look at us and see the disease's carriers."

"That's what the broadcasts say."

"The broadcasts say what's true."

"Maybe." Elias sat down across from her, taking her hands in his. "But maybe there's more to the truth than what fits on a Mesh screen. That's why they're sending observers, Mother. That's why they want people like me at the summit. To see for ourselves. To understand what we're dealing with."

Vera was quiet for a long moment. The kitchen hummed around them: the soft whir of the air processor, the gentle click of the heating unit, the distant pulse of the building's power grid. The sounds of home. The sounds of everything Elias had ever known.

"Wait here," she said finally. She rose and disappeared into the back of the apartment, into the room that had been his parents' bedroom and was now hers alone. When she returned, she was carrying something small, metallic, glinting in the apartment's steady light.

A compass. His father's compass.

"This was his," Vera said, placing it in Elias's palm. "He carried it on every expedition. Said it was the only thing he trusted completely, because it couldn't lie. Couldn't be reprogrammed or adjusted. It just pointed to where it pointed, no matter what anyone wanted it to say."

Elias turned the compass over in his hands. It was old, clearly, the brass casing worn smooth by decades of use. The needle trembled slightly, then steadied, pointing east. Toward home, he thought. Toward everything familiar.

"I want you to take it," Vera said. "So you can always find your way back. No matter how far you go. No matter what you see out there."

"Mother..."

"Promise me." Her voice cracked slightly. "Promise me you'll come home."

He closed his fingers around the compass, feeling its weight, its solidity. A piece of his father, carried across years and grief. A tether to the place he belonged.

"I promise," he said.

Vera embraced him then, holding on longer than usual, and Elias let her. He breathed in the familiar scent of her, the soap she had used since he was a child, the faint chemical undertone of the apartment's filtered air. When she finally let go, her eyes were dry, but her smile was fragile.

"Tell me everything," she said. "When you come back. I want to know what it's really like out there."

"I will," he said. "I'll tell you everything."

He stayed for dinner, eating the reconstituted vegetables and synthetic protein without really tasting them, listening to his mother talk about her work at the distribution center and her neighbors' small dramas. It was ordinary. Comfortable. The life he had always expected to live, stretching out before him in an unbroken line from birth to death.

But now there was a bend in that line. A place where the familiar path curved toward something unknown.

He walked home through the evening streets, the compass heavy in his pocket. The Mesh screens cycled through their nightly rotation: entertainment programs, productivity updates, weather forecasts for tomorrow's identical weather. Elias watched them without seeing, his mind already traveling west, toward the Frontier, toward the summit, toward the answers to questions he was only beginning to form.

* * *

Three days later, Elias boarded the diplomatic transport with eleven other members of the Pale Cities delegation.

The craft was military-grade, angular and imposing, its hull painted in the gray-and-silver livery of the Border Guard. Captain Lucian Ford met them at the boarding ramp, a tall man with close-cropped hair and eyes that seemed to register everything without reacting to any of it. He checked credentials, assigned compartments, and delivered a brief security orientation in a voice that made even routine procedures sound like matters of life and death.

Elias found his seat near the rear of the passenger compartment, next to a narrow window that offered a view of the launch platform. The other delegates settled around him: functionaries, advisors, security personnel, and near the front, the two figures who would lead the delegation at Threshold.

Councillor Aldric Vane was a heavy-set man with a politician's practiced smile and tired eyes. He had negotiated with the MNA before, years ago, and was said to believe that accommodation was possible if both sides were willing to make sacrifices. Some in the Assembly considered this view dangerously naive. Others called it pragmatic. Elias had no opinion; he had never met the man.

The other figure he recognized immediately, though they had never been introduced. Chief Doctrine Keeper Julienne Drax was small, precise, immaculately dressed in the formal gray of her office. Her hair was pulled back severely, and her face had the kind of controlled stillness that suggested either perfect calm or carefully contained intensity. She was, by all accounts, brilliant. She was also, by the same accounts, someone you did not want as an enemy.

She would be his direct superior for the duration of the summit. The thought made Elias's palms sweat.

The transport lifted off with a shudder and a roar, pressing him back into his seat. Through the window, he watched Nova-Providence fall away beneath them: the ordered ranks of towers, the geometric precision of the transit grid, the faint shimmer of the atmospheric processors along the city's edge. It looked, from above, like a diagram of itself. Perfect. Complete. A city that had solved the problem of how to live.

They climbed through the artificial sky, through the layer of processed air that kept Nova-Providence's climate stable and predictable, and then they were above it, and Elias saw something he had never seen before.

Clouds. Real clouds. Vast white structures piled on top of each other like mountains made of light, casting shadows that moved across the land below in patterns no algorithm had designed. The sky beyond them was blue, but not the calibrated blue of the atmospheric processors. This blue was deeper. Wilder. A color that seemed to go on forever.

Elias pressed his hand against the window, feeling the cold of the glass, the vibration of the engines. His father's compass was in his pocket, pointing steadily east, toward home. But home was behind him now, shrinking in the distance, and ahead there was only the unknown.

The transport flew west, toward the Frontier.

Below them, the land began to change. The cultivated zones around Nova-Providence gave way to industrial sectors, then to the buffer territories, then to something else entirely. Elias had studied maps of the Frontier, had seen the satellite images in his academy courses, but nothing had prepared him for the reality of it. The ruins spread across the landscape like wounds that had never healed: collapsed structures, rusted machinery, forests growing wild through the bones of abandoned settlements. This was what remained of the old world, before the Separation. Before the Pale Cities chose their path.

The official history said the ancestors had fled this devastation, had built something better in the east. But looking down at the ruins, Elias found himself wondering: devastation from what? The maps never said. The textbooks never explained. It was simply the chaos of the ungoverned lands, the natural result of the MNA's failure to impose proper order on their territory.

But the ruins looked old. Older than the Separation. And they didn't look like the result of chaos. They looked like the result of something deliberate. Something violent.

Elias pushed the thought away. He was tired. He was seeing things that weren't there. The briefing materials had warned about this: the Frontier had a way of playing tricks on the mind, making you question things that didn't need questioning. The important thing was to stay focused. To observe. To document.

To understand.

He pulled out his tablet and began reviewing his notes on MNA diplomatic protocols. The words blurred slightly as the transport shuddered through a patch of turbulence, but he kept reading. Kept preparing. Kept pushing down the small, insistent voice that wondered what else his education might have left unexplained.

Outside the window, the clouds thickened. For the first time in his life, Elias Harren could not predict the weather.

He found, to his surprise, that he didn't mind.

3

What the Wind Carries

Tower Seven sang in a voice that Aiyana was only beginning to understand.

She had arrived at the eastern station three days before the summit, assigned to the maintenance rotation as part of her new duties. It was standard protocol for junior engineers: before you could represent the Wind Spine network at diplomatic functions, you needed to know the network from the inside. And Tower Seven was the edge of that network, the last node before the Frontier swallowed everything into silence.

The tower rose from the ridge like a prayer made visible. Its central column was living wood, a species of oak that had been cultivated and shaped over eighty years into a spiral of impossible grace. Branches extended outward at precise intervals, each one strung with resonance fibers that caught the wind and translated its motion into harmonic energy. At dawn and dusk, when the thermals shifted, the whole structure hummed with a sound that was almost music, almost speech, almost something older than either.

Aiyana stood on the maintenance platform halfway up the

tower's height, her hands pressed against the warm bark of the central column. Through her palms, she could feel the pulse of the Bioweb beneath her, flowing through root systems that connected Tower Seven to every other node on the continent. Data moved through those roots: weather patterns, agricultural reports, the slow conversations of forest management systems. But it didn't feel like data. It felt like breathing.

"You're listening too hard."

Senior Engineer Tomas Brightwater stood behind her, his arms crossed, his weathered face creased with something between amusement and concern. He was old enough to have worked on Tower Seven when it was first grown, one of the original team who had shaped its early development. His bond-companion, a red-tailed hawk named Whisper, perched on a nearby branch, watching Aiyana with the mild curiosity of an animal who had seen many junior engineers come and go.

"I'm trying to understand the resonance patterns," Aiyana said. "The manuals describe them, but the descriptions don't match what I'm feeling."

"The manuals were written by people who understood the towers intellectually." Tomas moved to stand beside her, placing his own palm against the column. "Understanding them physically is different. You can't force it. The tower will teach you its rhythms when it's ready."

"That sounds like something Elder Nayeli would say."

"Where do you think she learned it?" A brief smile crossed his face. "Nayeli trained here, decades ago. So did your father, if I remember correctly. The eastern towers have a way of shaping people."

Aiyana looked out over the landscape below. The ridge fell away to the east in a tumble of rock and pine, eventually flattening into the brown expanse of the Frontier. From this height, she could see the boundary markers: tall posts of white stone, spaced at regular intervals, marking the line between the Many Nations Alliance and the ungoverned territories beyond. Past the markers, the land looked different. Grayer. Quieter. As if something essential had been drained from it.

"What's it like out there?" she asked. "The Frontier."

Tomas was quiet for a moment. "I went once, when I was younger. A salvage expedition to recover equipment from an abandoned station." He shook his head slowly. "The silence is the worst part. You don't realize how much you depend on the Bioweb until it's gone. Out there, you're alone in a way that's hard to describe. The land doesn't know you. The wind doesn't carry anything but dust."

"But people live there. Bridge-builders. Others."

"Some do." His voice was careful now. "Your brother, if the stories are true."

Aiyana turned to look at him. "You know about Kele?"

The question brought back another memory, sharp and unexpected: Kele's hands guiding hers against a younger tree, years ago, when she was still learning what the Bioweb could teach.

"You're trying to hear it," he'd said. *"That's your problem. The Bioweb doesn't speak. It breathes. You don't listen to breathing. You match it."*

She had been twelve, impatient, convinced that her older brother was speaking in riddles just to annoy her. But he'd kept her hands pressed to the bark until she'd stopped straining to hear and simply let herself feel. The pulse beneath her palms. The slow rhythm that had nothing to do with sound.

"There," he'd whispered when her breathing finally matched

27

the tree's. *"Now you're not listening. Now you're part of the conversation."*

It was the first lesson she'd truly understood. Years later, it was still the one she returned to whenever the Bioweb seemed silent, whenever the harmonics wouldn't resolve into meaning. Match the breathing. Become part of the conversation.

Kele had taught her that. And then he'd left to have conversations with people who had forgotten how to breathe at all.

"Everyone at Tower Seven knows about Kele Waketah. He worked here for two years before he left. Brilliant engineer. Maybe the best I ever trained." Tomas met her eyes steadily. "He asked me questions, too. Questions about the Frontier, about the people who lived in the gray places. I told him what I knew. I sometimes wonder if I should have told him less."

"You think you encouraged him to leave?"

"I think Kele was going to leave no matter what anyone said. Some people aren't built to stay inside boundaries." He paused, choosing his words. "He believed the Pale Cities weren't beyond saving. That if someone could just show them a different way, they might choose differently. It's a generous belief. Maybe even a noble one."

"But?"

"But the Pale Cities have had four hundred years to choose differently. At some point, belief becomes denial. Generosity becomes blindness." Tomas shrugged, a gesture that carried more weight than it should have. "I hope I'm wrong. I hope Kele finds what he's looking for out there. But hope isn't certainty, and the Frontier has swallowed better people than your brother."

They stood in silence for a while, the tower humming around them. Above, Sitala circled lazily, riding the thermals that rose from the ridge. Whisper watched her with professional interest, one hunter assessing another.

"The diplomatic delegation arrives tomorrow," Tomas said eventually. "You should rest. Whatever happens at that summit, the next few weeks are going to be exhausting."

Aiyana nodded, but she didn't move from the platform. She stayed until the sun touched the western peaks, watching the light change, feeling the tower's song shift as the evening thermals rose. Somewhere in the resonance, she thought she could almost hear her brother's voice, asking questions no one wanted to answer.

She wondered if he was asking them still.

* * *

The delegation arrived with the morning light.

Aiyana watched from the station's observation deck as the sky-craft descended, a graceful vessel of woven fibers and living wood that moved through the air like a bird rather than a machine. It settled onto the landing platform with barely a sound, its surface rippling as it adjusted to the shift from flight to rest. Even now, after years of study, she found the technology beautiful. It was one thing to understand how the craft worked, how the bio-resonant materials responded to pilot intention and atmospheric conditions. It was another to watch it happen, to see human ingenuity and natural process working in perfect concert.

The delegation disembarked: half a dozen figures in the formal dress of their respective nations, accompanied by assistants and advisors. But Aiyana's attention focused on one man who walked slightly apart from the others, his stride unhurried, his silver hair catching the morning sun.

Chogan Grayfeather. She recognized him from images, from

broadcasts, from her mother's stories about the old days when peace had seemed more possible. He was smaller than she had expected, his frame slight beneath the traditional robes of the Lake Nations. But there was something in the way he moved, a quality of attention, that made the space around him seem significant.

He was also, she realized, walking directly toward her.

"Aiyana Waketah." His voice was quiet but carried clearly, the voice of a man accustomed to being heard without raising his volume. "You have your father's eyes. And, I suspect, your brother's stubbornness."

She wasn't sure how to respond to that. "Elder Grayfeather. It's an honor."

"The honor is mutual. Nayeli speaks highly of you. She says you have an unusual gift for reading harmonic patterns." He studied her face with eyes that seemed to see more than they revealed. "I understand you completed your initiation flight last week. Through the Needle Pass."

"Yes, Elder."

"I failed that pass three times before I managed it." A faint smile. "Of course, I was never much of a flyer. My talents lie in other directions." He gestured toward the tower looming above them. "Will you walk with me? I'd like to see the eastern installation before the summit begins. It's been many years since I visited."

They walked together along the ridge path, Sitala gliding overhead. The other delegates had dispersed toward their quarters, attended by station staff, leaving Chogan and Aiyana in something approaching privacy. The tower's hum surrounded them, a constant presence that Aiyana was only now learning to tune out.

"You requested me for this assignment," Aiyana said. "My mother told me."

"I did."

"May I ask why?"

Chogan was quiet for several paces, his attention seemingly fixed on the path ahead. When he spoke, his voice had lost some of its formal cadence. "I knew your father. We worked together during the Second Boundary Talks, twenty years ago. He was a good man. Principled. He believed in the possibility of coexistence, even when the evidence suggested otherwise."

"He died believing that."

"Yes." The word carried weight. "The Tower Three incident. I was at the capital when the news came. It was... a difficult day." He paused. "I also knew your brother, Aiyana. Not as well as I knew your father, but well enough to recognize the same qualities. The same stubbornness. The same belief that understanding could bridge any divide."

Aiyana felt her chest tighten. "Do you know where he is?"

"I know where he was, six months ago. Deep in the Frontier, working with a community of mixed heritage. Settlers' descendants who chose not to join the Pale Cities. Bridge people, they call themselves. Neither one thing nor the other." Chogan's expression was difficult to read. "He was teaching them sustainable practices. Trying to show them that our way of life was possible, even outside Alliance territory."

"That sounds like Kele."

"It does. It also sounds dangerous." They had reached a point where the path curved around the tower's base, offering a panoramic view of the Frontier. Chogan stopped, his gaze fixed on the distant gray. "Your brother believes the Pale Cities can be healed. That their people are victims of their own history, trapped in patterns they might break if someone showed them how. It is a beautiful belief, Aiyana. It may also be a dangerous one."

"Dangerous how?"

"The Pale Cities do not want to be healed. Their leaders have spent centuries constructing a narrative that justifies their existence: they are the survivors, the strong ones, the people who refused to surrender to primitive ways. That narrative is their identity. Their power depends on it." Chogan turned to face her. "If Kele succeeds, if he shows that our way is possible for their people, he doesn't just threaten their policies. He threatens their entire understanding of who they are. There are those in the Pale Cities who would do anything to prevent that."

Aiyana thought of her brother, out there in the silence, teaching strangers how to grow food in harmony with the land. She thought of the Pale Cities delegation that would arrive at Threshold tomorrow, bringing their gray uniforms and their careful speeches. Two worlds, circling each other like wary animals, neither willing to look away.

"Why are you telling me this?" she asked.

"Because the summit will not go as planned." Chogan's voice was very quiet now. "I have been negotiating with the Pale Cities for thirty years. I know their patterns, their tells, the way they prepare the ground before making a move. Something is different this time. They are too eager. Too accommodating. It makes me uneasy."

"You think they're planning something."

"I think they always plan something. The question is what." He resumed walking, and Aiyana fell into step beside him. "I requested you for this delegation because I need people around me who can see clearly. Who are not so invested in the old grievances that they cannot recognize new threats. Your father had that quality. Your brother has it too, though it may have led him astray. I am hoping you have inherited it."

"I'm a junior engineer. I just finished my initiation."

"Yes. And at the summit, you will be a junior technical advisor, present to answer questions about Wind Spine operations and Bioweb protocols. That is your official role." Chogan's smile was thin but genuine. "Unofficially, I am asking you to watch. To listen. To notice things that others might dismiss. And if you see something that troubles you, tell me immediately. Can you do that?"

Aiyana looked at him: this old man with his quiet voice and his thirty years of failed negotiations, asking a newly certified engineer to be his eyes and ears at the most important diplomatic event in a generation. It should have felt absurd. Instead, it felt inevitable.

"I can do that," she said.

"Good." He placed a hand briefly on her shoulder, the gesture somehow both formal and fatherly. "Now. Show me this tower. I want to understand what we are protecting before we sit down to negotiate its future."

* * *

That night, Aiyana could not sleep.

She lay in her quarters at the tower base, listening to the sounds of the station settling around her. The soft hum of the environmental systems. The distant call of night birds. The ever-present undertone of the tower itself, singing its endless song to the wind.

Chogan's words circled in her mind.

Something is different this time. They are too eager.

She had spent the afternoon showing him the tower, explaining the resonance systems, demonstrating the calibration protocols. He had asked good questions, probing questions, the questions of someone who wanted to understand not just how things worked but why they might stop working. By the end, she had begun to see Tower Seven through new eyes: not just as a marvel of engineering, but as a vulnerability. A point of failure that the wrong people might exploit.

Outside her window, Sitala perched on the designated roost, her golden feathers silver in the starlight. Through the bond, Aiyana could feel the eagle's contentment: belly full, night calm, no threats in the darkness. It was a simple feeling, an animal feeling, and it should have been comforting.

But something else was there too. Something Aiyana couldn't quite identify.

She rose from her bed and moved to the window, pressing her palm against the glass. The tower's hum was stronger here, conducted through the station's walls, and she let herself sink into it. Felt the harmonics move through her bones. Let her awareness spread outward, the way Tomas had shown her, following the resonance patterns into the larger network.

The Bioweb unfolded before her like a map drawn in sound. She could sense the other towers on the ridge, their songs interweaving with Tower Seven's. She could feel the data streams flowing beneath the earth, the constant pulse of information that kept the Alliance connected. It was beautiful. It was home.

And somewhere in it, there was a wrongness.

She couldn't pinpoint it. Couldn't name it. It was like hearing a single flat note in a symphony, a frequency that didn't quite belong. Every time she tried to focus on it, it slipped away, lost in the larger harmony. But it was there. She was certain of it.

Or was she? She was exhausted. She was anxious about the summit. She had spent the day with a legendary diplomat who had all but told her that disaster was coming. Maybe her mind was inventing threats where none existed. Maybe she was hearing her own fear echoing back at her.

She withdrew from the network, pulling her awareness back into her body. The room felt smaller now, more solid. Sitala stirred on her perch, sensing Aiyana's unease, and sent a wordless query through the bond:

Danger?

I don't know, Aiyana thought back. *Maybe. I don't know.*

The eagle settled, accepting the uncertainty with the patience of a predator who knew that waiting was often the wisest response to the unknown. Aiyana envied her that patience. She wished she could simply perch and wait, trusting that clarity would come.

Instead, she returned to bed and lay staring at the ceiling, listening to the tower sing.

Somewhere in the song, a note was wrong.

Somewhere in the darkness, something was waiting.

And in three days, the summit would begin.

4

The Observer's Eye

History, Julienne Drax had learned long ago, was not about truth. It was about survival.

She sat in her private cabin aboard the diplomatic transport, reviewing the materials she had prepared for the summit. Documents spread across her work surface in careful arrangement: primary sources, secondary analyses, talking points. Each piece selected and positioned to tell a specific story. Not a false story. Julienne never lied, not in the crude sense. She simply understood that facts were raw material, and raw material required shaping.

The MNA would come to Threshold with their own version of events. They would speak of stolen lands and broken promises. And their version would be compelling, because it contained elements of truth, and truth was always more dangerous than fiction.

A chime sounded at her cabin door. "Enter."

Councillor Aldric Vane stepped inside, his heavy frame filling the doorway. Strong jaw, tired eyes, the look of someone who had seen too much and kept going. The public adored him.

Julienne found him useful but exhausting.

"Keeper Drax. I wanted to discuss the opening session." He settled into the chair across from her. "I've reviewed your historical presentation. It's thorough. Compelling, even. But it's aggressive. If we open with accusations of MNA technological instability, we put them on the defensive before we've begun."

"That is the intention."

"Is it?" Vane's eyes searched her face. "I thought the intention was to establish grounds for cooperation. To begin the process of normalization."

Julienne set down her documents. "Councillor, may I speak frankly?"

"I would prefer it."

"The MNA does not want normalization. They want submission. Every concession we make, they interpret as weakness." She kept her voice even, almost gentle. "Accommodation is not possible with people who consider your existence an error."

"You don't know that."

"I have spent my career studying them. They are not monsters, Councillor. They are true believers. And true believers cannot compromise, because compromise requires admitting that the other side might have a point."

Vane was quiet for a long moment. "What outcome do you expect from this summit?"

"Stalemate. Mutual recrimination. A hardening of positions." She allowed herself a thin smile. "But stalemate is not defeat. Stalemate is time. And time is what we need."

"Time for what?"

"To become strong enough that accommodation is no longer necessary."

The words hung in the air. Vane's face went through several expressions before settling on resignation. He knew she was right. He simply didn't want to live in a world where that was true.

"I hope you're wrong," he said, rising. "I hope there's more possibility in that room than you're allowing for."

"So do I, Councillor. Truly."

And in that moment, she meant it.

* * *

The encrypted channel opened at midnight, as scheduled.

Julienne sat alone in her cabin, the lights dimmed, her terminal displaying only a blank screen with a blinking cursor. The channel was routed through fourteen different nodes, encrypted with protocols that would take the MNA's best analysts years to crack. Even so, she kept her words minimal.

Text appeared, letter by letter: *STATUS?*

She typed: *EN ROUTE. DELEGATION PREPARED. VANE REMAINS OPTIMISTIC.*

A pause. Then: *OPTIMISM IS USEFUL. DISAPPOINTMENT SHARPENS RESOLVE.*

The Choir understood human nature. Vane's optimism would be useful. When the summit failed, his disappointment would make him more receptive to alternative approaches.

THE DEVICE? she typed.

IN PLACE. CALIBRATION COMPLETE. AWAITING AUTHORIZATION.

TIMELINE?

DEPENDENT ON SUMMIT OUTCOME. IF TALKS COLLAPSE NATURALLY, DEMONSTRATION UNNECESSARY. IF ACCOMMODATION APPEARS POSSIBLE, DEMONSTRATION WILL ENSURE COLLAPSE.

The plan was elegant in its flexibility. If the summit failed on its own, the device would remain dormant. But if Vane some-how found common ground with the MNA, the Choir would act. Would create an incident that made peace impossible.

She should have felt reassured. Instead, she felt unease.

WHAT KIND OF DEMONSTRATION? she typed.

A long pause. Longer than the encryption lag could explain. Then:

THE KIND THAT REMINDS THEM WHAT SILENCE FEELS LIKE.

The channel closed. Julienne stared at the blank screen, her reflection ghostly in the dark glass.

She had worked with the Choir for five years, had provided them intelligence, had helped shape the conditions that made their work possible. But she had never asked for details about their methods. She had not wanted to know.

The MNA's technology was built on connection. Their Bioweb, their Wind Spines, their living cities. All of it depended on organic systems talking to organic systems in harmonies that Pale City engineers could barely comprehend. It was impressive. It was also vulnerable in ways the MNA themselves seemed not to understand.

The kind that reminds them what silence feels like.

Julienne closed her terminal and sat in the dark for a long time. She told herself it was necessary. That the MNA's response would reveal their true nature, would justify everything the Pale Cities had done and would do.

She almost believed it.

In a few hours, she would sit across from them and pretend to negotiate. Would present her evidence, plant seeds of doubt, establish that the Pale Cities had a voice that could not simply be dismissed.

And somewhere in the background, the Choir would wait.

39

Their device ready. Their patience infinite.

Julienne Drax had spent her life learning how to tell stories.

She was very, very good at it.

5

Tower Seven

The wrongness woke her before the alarms did.

Aiyana came out of sleep like a swimmer breaking surface, gasping, her heart already racing before her mind caught up. The quarters were dark, the station quiet, but something was screaming at the edge of her awareness. Not a sound. A sensation. The harmonic equivalent of fingernails dragged across glass.

She was on her feet and moving before she fully understood why. Through the window, Sitala had launched from her perch, her silhouette cutting across the star-field in agitated circles. The bond between them thrummed with the eagle's distress:

wrong wrong wrong something wrong

Then the alarms began.

They were not the sharp electronic wails of Pale City emergency systems. They were organic, grown into the station's walls, and they keened like wounded animals. Aiyana had heard alarm tones in training simulations, but nothing had prepared her for the sound of a living system crying out in pain.

She ran.

The corridors were chaos. Other engineers stumbled from their quarters, faces slack with confusion and fear. Someone was shouting about the resonance monitors. Someone else was calling for Senior Engineer Brightwater. Aiyana pushed through them, following the pull in her chest, the wrongness that grew stronger with every step toward the tower's base.

The control center was a storm of activity. Banks of living displays pulsed with colors she had never seen in any manual, frequencies visualized as angry reds and sickly yellows. Tomas Brightwater stood at the central console, his weathered face pale, his hands moving across the interface with desperate precision.

"What's happening?" Aiyana reached his side, scanning the displays. The data made no sense. The tower's harmonics were oscillating wildly, cycling through frequencies that should have been impossible. "This looks like interference, but the patterns don't match any natural phenomenon."

"Because it's not natural." Tomas's voice was tight. "Something is disrupting the resonance externally. I've never seen anything like it."

"Can we compensate?"

"I'm trying." His fingers danced across the interface, adjusting frequencies, attempting to find counter-harmonics that might stabilize the system. "The tower's trying to adapt, but the interference keeps shifting. It's like it's learning our responses."

Aiyana stared at the displays, her mind racing. The patterns were chaotic, but there was structure beneath the chaos. A rhythm. Almost like a heartbeat, if the heart were sick and stuttering.

"Let me try something." She pushed past him to a secondary

console, calling up the raw harmonic data. The numbers scrolled faster than she could consciously process, but she wasn't trying to read them. She was trying to

feel them, the way Tomas had taught her to feel the tower's song.

There. Beneath the chaos, a carrier frequency. Something artificial, something that didn't belong to any natural system she had ever encountered. It was threading through the tower's harmonics like a virus through blood, turning the body against itself.

"I found it," she breathed. "There's an external signal. If I can isolate the frequency, maybe we can filter it out."

"Do it."

She worked frantically, her fingers finding keys she barely remembered learning to use. The isolation protocols were designed for natural interference, for solar events and atmospheric disturbances. She had to modify them on the fly, adjusting parameters, narrowing the filter band, trying to catch the invasive signal without disrupting the harmonics it had already contaminated.

For a moment, she thought she had it. The oscillations began to stabilize. The angry colors on the displays shifted toward yellow, toward green.

Then the signal changed.

It shifted frequencies faster than her filter could track, jumping across the spectrum in patterns that seemed almost intelligent. Every adjustment she made, it countered. Every compensation, it overwhelmed. She was fighting something that could think, that could adapt, that had been designed specifically to defeat the defenses she was trying to build.

"It's not working." Her voice cracked. "Tomas, it's not

working. The signal is adaptive."

"Everyone out." His voice cut through the chaos, suddenly calm in the way that truly frightened people sometimes became. "Everyone out of the tower. Now."

"We can still try to stabilize the core resonance. If we can just hold it long enough for the network to compensate, the other towers might be able to take the load."

"Look at the structural readings, Aiyana."

She looked. And she understood.

The living wood of the tower's central column was dying. The harmonic disruption wasn't just affecting the resonance systems. It was killing the tower itself, cell by cell, the same way a sound at the right frequency could shatter glass. The displays showed the damage spreading upward from the base, climbing through the spiral structure like disease through a body.

Tower Seven was not malfunctioning. Tower Seven was being murdered.

"Go," Tomas said. He was already at the data terminal, his fingers moving with terrible purpose. "I need to save what I can of the records. The network needs to know what happened here."

"I'm not leaving you."

"You are. That's an order." He didn't look at her. His attention was fixed on the terminal, on the data streaming past, on the last moments of a tower he had helped raise from a seedling eighty years ago. "Someone needs to survive this. Someone who understands what they saw. Go. Now. Take the backup archive."

He thrust a data chip into her hand. She took it without thinking, her body responding to his authority even as her mind rebelled.

"Tomas."

"Go."

She ran.

* * *

The station was emptying, people streaming toward the emergency shelters on the ridge's far side. Aiyana pushed against the current, moving toward the exit that would bring her closest to Sitala's position. She could feel the eagle circling above, feel her panic and confusion and the fierce imperative to

fly, escape, survive.

She burst through the exterior doors into the predawn darkness. The tower loomed above her, its spiral form silhouetted against the stars, and even in the dim light she could see that something was wrong. The living wood was trembling, its branches swaying in patterns that had nothing to do with the wind. The resonance fibers were snapping one by one, their delicate strands fraying like overtightened strings.

Sitala dove out of the darkness, her cry piercing the chaos. She didn't land on Aiyana's shoulder. She raked her talons across Aiyana's arm, drawing blood, pulling her sideways with frantic urgency.

MOVE

Aiyana moved.

She threw herself to the left, rolling down a small embankment, feeling stones and roots tear at her clothes. Behind her, exactly where she had been standing, a massive branch crashed to the ground. It was followed by another. And another. The tower was coming apart.

She scrambled to her feet and ran, Sitala screaming overhead, guiding her through the falling debris with warnings that came faster than thought. Left. Right. Duck. Jump. The world became a blur of motion and terror, her body responding to the eagle's commands before her conscious mind could process them.

The sound was the worst part. Not the crash of falling wood, not the screams of people still too close to the structure. The sound was the tower itself, its death cry. Eighty years of growth, of cultivation, of careful shaping by generations of engineers, ending in a harmony of destruction. The resonance fibers sang as they snapped, each one adding its voice to a chord that grew more discordant with every passing second.

Aiyana reached the ridge crest and turned back, unable to look away.

Tower Seven fell.

It did not collapse the way a Pale City structure would have collapsed, in an avalanche of steel and concrete. It came apart organically, the spiral unraveling, the branches spreading outward like fingers reaching for something they would never grasp. The central column cracked along fault lines that followed the grain of the living wood, and then it split, and then it was falling, and then it was gone.

The impact shook the ground beneath her feet. Dust and debris billowed outward in a great wave, carrying with it the scent of sap and soil and something else, something like burning. The Bioweb convulsed. Aiyana felt it through the soles of her feet, through the data chip clutched in her bleeding hand, through every cell of her body that had been trained to listen for the network's voice.

The network was screaming.

Connections severed. Data streams collapsed. The other

towers on the ridge were struggling to compensate, their harmonics shifting desperately to fill the gap where Tower Seven had been. But the gap was too large, the loss too sudden. The network had been designed for gradual change, for organic adaptation. It had not been designed for murder.

Aiyana sank to her knees in the dirt, the data chip still clutched in her hand. Sitala landed beside her, pressing close, her feathers brushing against Aiyana's cheek. Through the bond came a wordless comfort, an animal certainty:

Alive. We are alive. That is enough.

But it wasn't enough. Because Aiyana could see, in the settling dust, figures moving toward the ruins. Could hear voices calling names. Could count, with growing horror, the people who were not answering.

Tomas. Lira, the young engineer who had shared dinner with her two nights ago. Old Maren, who had been working the night shift in the calibration room. Fourteen voices that would never speak again, fourteen lives erased in the time it took a tower to fall.

And their companions. Whisper, Tomas's hawk, who had watched Aiyana with mild curiosity just yesterday. The bonded animals who had nested in the tower's branches, who had been part of its living system. They were gone too. The bonds severed so suddenly that Aiyana had felt the echo of it through the network, a chorus of small deaths adding their voices to the larger silence.

She pressed her forehead to the ground and wept.

* * *

Dawn came slowly, as if the sun itself was reluctant to illuminate what had happened.

Aiyana sat on the ridge crest where she had watched the tower

47

fall, wrapped in a thermal blanket someone had pressed into her hands. The data chip was still in her grip, its edges cutting into her palm. She had not let go of it. She was not sure she could.

The ruins spread below her, vast and incomprehensible. Where Tower Seven had stood for eighty years, there was now only wreckage. The living wood was already beginning to decay, the cellular structure that had maintained it breaking down without the harmonic energy that had sustained it. By tomorrow, it would be gray and brittle. By next week, it would be indistinguishable from the ancient ruins that littered the Frontier.

Rescue teams moved through the debris, searching for survivors. They would not find many. The collapse had been too sudden, too complete. The people who had escaped had done so in the first minutes, when the alarms gave them warning. The people who had stayed, trying to save the tower, trying to save each other, had died with it.

Chogan Grayfeather found her there as the sun crested the eastern peaks.

He did not speak. He simply sat down beside her on the cold ground, his formal robes dusty and disheveled, and looked out at what remained of Tower Seven. For a long time, there was only the sound of the wind and the distant calls of the rescue teams.

"It wasn't a malfunction," Aiyana said finally. Her voice sounded strange to her own ears, hollow and distant. "There was an external signal. Something designed to disrupt the harmonics. The tower didn't fail. It was attacked."

"I know." Chogan's voice was heavy with a weariness that went beyond physical exhaustion. "Our analysts are already reviewing the network data. The signature is unlike anything in our records."

"The Pale Cities."

"Almost certainly. Though proving it will be another matter." He paused. "The summit begins in three days. At Threshold. There will be pressure to cancel, to respond with force, to abandon diplomacy entirely. Some of that pressure will be justified."

Aiyana turned to look at him. His face was drawn, aged overnight by grief and responsibility. She remembered what he had told her just yesterday:

Something is different this time. They are too eager.

He had known. Not what would happen, but that something would. And he had been unable to stop it.

"What do we do?" she asked.

"We go to the summit." His voice was quiet but certain. "We sit across from the people who did this, and we do not give them the war they want. We document what happened here. We present our evidence. And we make them understand that we know what they've done."

"That's not justice."

"No. It's survival." He reached over and gently uncurled her fingers from around the data chip. "Is this what I think it is?"

"Tomas gave it to me. The backup archive. Everything the tower recorded before it fell." Her voice broke slightly. "He died saving it."

Chogan held the chip carefully, reverently, as if it were something sacred. "Then his death was not meaningless. This is evidence. This is proof. This is the truth of what was done here."

He rose, slowly, his joints stiff from sitting on the cold ground.

"Come. There is work to do. Preparations to make. The summit will proceed, and you will be there with me."

"Why?" The question came out as almost a whisper. "Why do you still want me there? I couldn't save the tower. I couldn't save anyone."

Chogan looked down at her, and something in his expression shifted. Not pity, exactly. Something harder. Something that expected more from her than she felt capable of giving.

"You recognized the attack for what it was. You identified the carrier frequency when engineers with decades more experience were still trying to understand the malfunction. You saved the data that may be our only proof of what happened." He held out his hand to help her rise. "You did not fail, Aiyana. You survived. And now you must do something harder."

"What?"

"Bear witness. Remember what you saw. And when the time comes, speak the truth to people who have built their entire world on lies."

She took his hand and let him pull her to her feet. Her body ached. Her heart ached worse. But somewhere beneath the grief, she felt something else stirring. Not anger, exactly. Not yet. Something quieter. Something that would grow.

Behind her, the sun rose over the ruins of Tower Seven, casting long shadows across the wreckage. Sitala circled overhead, her golden feathers catching the light, her presence in Aiyana's mind a steady anchor against the chaos.

In three days, she would sit across from the people who had done this.

In three days, she would look into their eyes and know them for what they were.

And she would remember Tomas Brightwater, pressing a

data chip into her hand as the tower died around him. Would remember Whisper, circling above a structure that would soon be her grave. Would remember the sound of fourteen voices falling silent, one by one, as the network screamed.

She would remember everything.

And she would make them answer for it.

6

The Message That Wasn't Sent

Threshold was not what Elias had expected.

The observatory complex rose from the Frontier like a dream of what might have been. Its architecture was hybrid, impossible: MNA organic curves flowing into Pale City steel reinforcements, living wood wrapped around metal frameworks, windows of glass set into walls that seemed to breathe. It should have looked chaotic, a collision of incompatible philosophies. Instead, it looked like a conversation. A question that had never quite been answered.

The transport settled onto the landing platform with a mechanical shudder, and Elias pressed his face to the window like a child. He had studied images of Threshold in preparation for the summit, had read the historical accounts of its construction during the Brief Cooperation Era, had memorized the diplomatic protocols that governed its neutral status. None of it had prepared him for the reality of standing on ground that belonged to neither world.

"Harren." Keeper Drax's voice cut through his reverie. "Stop gawking. We have work to do."

He turned to find her already moving toward the transport's exit, her document case in hand, her posture radiating controlled purpose. The other delegates were gathering their belongings, arranging themselves in the informal hierarchy that would govern their movements for the next several days. Councillor Vane at the front, flanked by his senior advisors. Keeper Drax a step behind, her position ambiguous but her authority unmistakable. Captain Lucian Ford and his security detail bringing up the rear, their gray uniforms and watchful eyes a reminder that diplomacy, in the end, was backed by force.

Elias fell into line near the back, where junior attachés belonged. His tablet was clutched against his chest, loaded with the documentation protocols he had memorized on the flight. He was ready. He was prepared. He was exactly where he had always wanted to be.

So why did he feel like he was walking into something he didn't understand?

The delegation disembarked into pale morning light. The air tasted different here, Elias noticed immediately. Cleaner. Sharper. Without the faint metallic undertone that he had never consciously registered in Nova-Providence but now, in its absence, recognized as the taste of home. He breathed deeply, filling his lungs with something that felt almost like freedom.

A Threshold administrator met them at the platform's edge, a middle-aged woman with the neutral dress and careful expression of someone who had spent her career navigating between hostile powers. She welcomed them in formal phrases, directed them toward their assigned quarters, explained the schedule for the day's preliminary sessions. Elias listened with half his attention, the other half absorbed by the world around him.

The observatory grounds were beautiful in a way that made him ache. Gardens that seemed to have grown rather than been planted. Pathways that curved in patterns suggesting purpose rather than geometry. Birds he didn't recognize calling from trees that shouldn't have been able to survive this far into the Frontier. It was as if someone had taken the best of what the MNA could build and the best of what the Pale Cities could engineer and merged them into something neither could achieve alone.

He was so absorbed in looking that he almost missed the moment everything changed.

* * *

The message arrived as they were settling into their quarters.

Elias was unpacking his document case, arranging his materials on the small desk that had been provided, when he heard the commotion in the corridor. Raised voices. Footsteps moving with urgent purpose. The kind of controlled chaos that meant something had gone very wrong.

He stepped into the hallway and found Captain Ford striding past, his face set in an expression of focused calm that somehow communicated alarm more effectively than panic would have. Two of his officers followed close behind, speaking in low, rapid tones.

"What's happening?" Elias asked, falling into step beside one of the officers, a young woman with lieutenant's insignia.

She glanced at him, assessed his junior status, and apparently decided he was harmless enough to answer. "MNA emergency communication. One of their installations collapsed overnight. Major casualties."

"Collapsed? What kind of installation?"

"One of those tower things. The ones that capture wind." She shook her head. "Details are still coming in. The Captain wants to assess how this affects our security posture."

She moved on, leaving Elias standing in the corridor with a strange weight settling into his chest. A Wind Spine tower. He had studied them in his cultural surveys, had marveled at the engineering that allowed living wood to capture and convert atmospheric energy. They were supposed to be nearly indestructible, designed to withstand centuries of use. For one to simply collapse...

He made his way to the delegation's common room, where the senior members had already gathered. Councillor Vane stood by the window, his heavy shoulders slumped, his face gray with what looked like genuine distress. Two of his advisors were speaking in hushed tones near the door. And Keeper Drax...

Keeper Drax sat in a high-backed chair, perfectly composed, reviewing documents on her tablet as if nothing unusual had occurred.

"This changes everything," Vane was saying to no one in particular. "Fourteen dead. Maybe more. Their entire eastern network destabilized. They'll be looking for someone to blame."

"They'll blame us regardless," one of his advisors replied. "They always do."

"Perhaps. But there's a difference between reflexive accusation and genuine suspicion." Vane turned from the window, his tired eyes sweeping the room. "We need to express our condolences. Formally. Immediately. Show them that we understand the magnitude of what's happened."

"I would advise caution." Drax's voice was cool, measured. She didn't look up from her tablet. "Excessive sympathy may be interpreted as guilt. We should express appropriate regret while maintaining our position that this tragedy, however unfortunate, is an internal MNA matter."

"People are dead, Keeper."

"People are always dead, Councillor. The question is how their deaths serve the living." Now she looked up, and Elias caught something in her expression that made him deeply uncomfortable. Not satisfaction, exactly. But not surprise either. "The summit will proceed. The MNA will present their evidence of the collapse. We will respond with our historical analysis of their technological vulnerabilities. The narrative writes itself."

Vane stared at her for a long moment, his face cycling through emotions too quickly to read. Then he turned back to the window, his shoulders set in a posture of weary resignation.

"Prepare a statement of condolence," he said quietly. "Brief. Formal. Sincere. I want it delivered to the MNA delegation within the hour."

"Councillor..."

"That's an order, Keeper."

The silence that followed was brittle enough to shatter. Drax held Vane's gaze for several seconds, something unspoken passing between them. Then she inclined her head, the barest acknowledgment of his authority, and returned to her tablet.

Elias backed out of the room, feeling as if he had witnessed something he shouldn't have. The corridor outside was empty now, the earlier commotion subsided into tense quiet. He leaned against the wall, trying to process what he had seen.

Drax had known. He was almost certain of it. Not the details, perhaps, but the shape of things. She had been too calm, too prepared with her response. Her talk of narratives writing themselves had sounded less like analysis than like script.

But that was impossible. Wasn't it? The Pale Cities were many things, but they weren't murderers. They didn't destroy infrastructure and kill civilians to gain diplomatic advantage. That was the kind of thing the MNA accused them of in propaganda broadcasts, the kind of paranoid fantasy that justified the endless tension between their peoples.

Elias pressed his palm against his chest, feeling his father's compass through the fabric of his jacket. East. Home. Everything familiar and true.

He pushed the thought away. He was tired. He was overwhelmed. He was reading meaning into coincidence because the alternative was too terrible to contemplate.

He had work to do. Documentation to prepare. A summit to observe.

He would focus on that. He would do his job. He would stop asking questions that had no good answers.

* * *

The reception that evening was supposed to be a formality.

Both delegations would gather in Threshold's central hall, exchange pleasantries, establish the personal connections that might smooth the way for tomorrow's official negotiations. It was theater, Elias understood. Carefully choreographed performance designed to create the appearance of good faith. He had read the protocols. He knew his role: observe, document, stay out of the way.

What the protocols hadn't prepared him for was the MNA.

They arrived as a group, entering the hall through doors that seemed to open of their own accord. Their clothing was unlike anything Elias had seen outside of historical archives: flowing fabrics in deep earth tones, embroidered with patterns that suggested meaning he couldn't decipher, cut in styles that managed to look both ancient and utterly contemporary. They moved differently than the Pale City delegates, he noticed. Less rigidly. More aware of each other and the space around them.

And their faces. Their faces were what struck him most.

He had grown up seeing MNA citizens in educational materials, in propaganda broadcasts, in the occasional news footage that made it through the Signal Mesh filters. They had always seemed somehow other. Exotic at best, primitive at worst. The images had taught him to see them as representatives of a failed way of life, people who had chosen stagnation over progress.

The people in front of him were none of those things. They were simply people. Tired, grieving, determined people who had traveled to this neutral ground to try to prevent a war. The woman with silver-streaked hair who must be Elder Blackriver had the same weary set to her shoulders that Councillor Vane carried. The tall man with the hawk-sharp face who had to be Commander Speaks-Low watched the Pale City delegation with the same assessing vigilance that Captain Ford employed.

They were not so different. That was the thought that kept surfacing, no matter how many times Elias tried to push it down. Strip away the clothing and the architecture and the technology, and they were all just people. Frightened people, trying to protect what they loved.

And then he saw her.

She stood near the back of the MNA delegation, younger than most of the others, her dark hair pulled back from a face that bore the marks of recent grief. Her eyes were red-rimmed, her posture held together by visible effort. She wore the same earth-toned clothing as her colleagues, but on her it looked less like traditional dress and more like armor. Something to hide behind.

She was beautiful. That was his first thought, and he immediately felt ashamed of it. She was also angry. That was his second thought, and it felt closer to the truth. She was looking at the Pale City delegation with an expression that combined exhaustion and rage in equal measure, as if she knew something about them that they didn't know about themselves.

As if she knew what Keeper Drax had almost certainly known this morning, when she sat in her chair and talked about narratives writing themselves.

Their eyes met across the room. Just for a moment. Just long enough for Elias to see the question forming in her face:

Do you know what your people did?

He looked away first. He had to. Because the answer to that question was becoming harder to avoid, and he wasn't ready to face it. Not yet. Not here, surrounded by people who expected him to play his role, to document their performance, to believe the story he had been raised to believe.

The reception proceeded according to protocol. Pleasantries were exchanged. Condolences were formally offered and formally accepted. Councillor Vane and the silver-haired elder spoke briefly, their conversation too quiet to overhear. Keeper Drax circulated among the MNA delegates with practiced grace, her smile revealing nothing.

Elias documented it all, his tablet capturing notes he would later organize into proper reports. But his attention kept drifting back to the young woman with the angry eyes. She didn't speak to anyone from the Pale City delegation. She barely spoke to anyone at all. She simply stood, and watched, and waited.

He wanted to approach her. To say something. To ask her name, to express condolences that actually meant something, to find out what she had seen that made her look at his people with such weary fury.

He didn't. He stayed in his place, played his role, documented the theater.

But he would remember her face. He was certain of that. He would remember the question in her eyes, and he would not be able to stop himself from trying to find the answer.

* * *

Later that night, alone in his quarters, Elias reviewed Keeper Drax's summit materials.

It was part of his assignment: to familiarize himself with all documentation before the formal sessions began. The materials were comprehensive, meticulously organized, exactly what he would have expected from someone of Drax's reputation. Historical analyses. Technical assessments. Visual aids designed to support each point in the Pale Cities' opening presentation.

The presentation focused on MNA technological vulnerabilities. Instances of system failures. Documented cases where their organic approach had produced inconsistent or unreliable results. It was, Elias had to admit, compelling. The evidence seemed solid. The conclusions seemed reasonable.

But something nagged at him as he scrolled through the files.

He stopped at a section titled "Historical Precedents for Wind Spine Instability." Three incidents were cited, each one supporting the argument that MNA technology was inherently prone to catastrophic failure. The citations were properly formatted, referencing archive documents and technical reports that Elias, as a cultural documentarian, should theoretically be able to verify.

He pulled up the Doctrine Hall archive access on his tablet

and searched for the first citation. Nothing. The document didn't exist, or at least didn't exist under the reference number provided.

A clerical error, probably. He searched for the second citation. Same result.

The third citation did appear in the archive, but when Elias pulled up the document, his stomach tightened. The report was about a Wind Spine tower, yes. But it didn't describe a failure. It described what the archive called a "reclamation attempt": Pale City forces had tried to seize control of the tower and been repelled by MNA defenders.

The report had been modified. He could see it in the version history: changes made three days before the summit, transforming an account of Pale City aggression into evidence of MNA technological weakness.

Elias stared at the screen, his hands trembling slightly.

It could be a mistake. It could be an oversight. It could be that he was misreading something, that his limited access was showing him incomplete information, that there was a perfectly reasonable explanation for why Keeper Drax's presentation cited documents that either didn't exist or said the opposite of what she claimed.

It could be a lot of things.

But the woman's face kept appearing in his mind. The question in her eyes.

Do you know what your people did?

He closed the files. Shut down his tablet. Sat in the darkness of his quarters, listening to the unfamiliar sounds of Threshold settling around him.

His father's compass was heavy in his pocket. He pulled it out, held it in his palm, watched the needle tremble and steady.

East. Home. Everything he had been taught to believe.

But home was starting to feel very far away. And the needle, he realized, pointed toward Nova-Providence. Toward the Doctrine Halls where documents could be modified three days before a summit. Toward a society that might have done something terrible and then rewritten history to hide it.

Toward everything he had always trusted, now trembling on the edge of collapse.

He put the compass away. Lay down on the unfamiliar bed. Closed his eyes.

Sleep did not come.

7

Accusations Without Evidence

Chogan Grayfeather had spent thirty years learning to read the silences between words.

He stood at the entrance to Threshold's summit chamber, watching the delegations arrange themselves on opposite sides of the great circular table. The room had been designed for moments like this: neutral ground rendered in neutral colors, the lighting calibrated to flatter no one and offend no one, the acoustics tuned to carry every word with equal clarity. It was a space that promised fairness. Chogan had learned, over three decades of negotiation, that such spaces often delivered the opposite.

The Pale Cities delegation had arrived first, a calculated move that allowed them to claim the seats facing the windows. It was a small advantage, forcing the MNA representatives to squint into the morning light, but Chogan noted it nonetheless. Keeper Drax, he suspected. She had a talent for these minor cruelties.

He moved to his own seat at the table's center, flanked by Elder Winona Blackriver and Commander Talon Speaks-Low. Behind him, in the observer chairs reserved for junior advisors, sat Aiyana Waketah. He had positioned her there deliberately, where she could see everything without being expected to speak. Where she could watch Keeper Drax's face when the evidence was presented.

The formalities began. Greetings were exchanged. The Threshold administrator read the protocols governing the session: equal speaking time, no interruptions, all statements to be recorded for official archives. Chogan listened with the fraction of his attention that such rituals required, the rest focused on the people across the table.

Councillor Vane looked tired. Genuinely tired, not the performed exhaustion of a politician seeking sympathy. The man had not slept well, and Chogan found himself wondering why. Guilt? Foreknowledge? Or simply the weight of representing a nation that might have just committed an act of war?

Keeper Drax, by contrast, looked immaculate. Her gray uniform was pressed to perfection, her hair arranged with mathematical precision, her expression a mask of professional courtesy. She met Chogan's eyes briefly, and in that moment he saw nothing. No triumph. No anxiety. No humanity at all. Just the smooth surface of someone who had learned to hide everything that mattered.

"Elder Grayfeather." The administrator's voice cut through his observations. "The Many Nations Alliance has requested to present first. You may proceed."

Chogan rose, feeling the familiar weight of responsibility settle onto his shoulders. He had given hundreds of presentations in rooms like this. Had argued for peace when war seemed inevitable, had negotiated compromises that satisfied no one but prevented catastrophe, had learned to speak truth to people who had built their lives on lies. None of it had prepared him for this moment.

Because this time, he had evidence. And evidence, he knew, was the most dangerous thing a diplomat could possess.

* * *

"Three days ago," he began, "Wind Spine Tower Seven collapsed. Fourteen of our people died. The eastern section of our continental network was destabilized. The environmental and infrastructural damage will take years to fully assess."

He paused, letting the words settle into the room's careful silence. Across the table, Councillor Vane's expression tightened. Keeper Drax remained utterly still.

"We are not here to assign blame." Chogan kept his voice measured, almost gentle. "We are here to present evidence. To share what we have learned about how and why this disaster occurred. And to invite our colleagues from the Pale Cities to help us understand what we have found."

He activated the display system, projecting harmonic data onto the chamber's central screen. The patterns meant nothing to most of the people in the room, he knew. But they would mean something to the technical advisors. And they would be part of the official record.

"These are the resonance readings from Tower Seven in the hours before the collapse. Normal operation shows stable harmonic patterns within expected parameters." He advanced the display. "At 3:47 in the morning, an external signal began disrupting those patterns. The signal was adaptive, shifting frequencies to counter our engineers' attempts at stabilization. Within eighteen minutes, the tower's living structure had sustained fatal damage."

He let the data speak for itself. The pattern of interference was clear to anyone with technical training: not a natural phenomenon, not a system malfunction, but a deliberate attack using technology designed specifically to destroy harmonic resonance systems.

"We do not possess technology capable of producing such a signal," Chogan continued. "Our systems are designed for harmony, not disruption. The frequency patterns suggest an approach to energy manipulation that is fundamentally different from our own. An approach that prioritizes control over cooperation. Extraction over integration."

He did not say

your approach. He did not need to. The implication hung in the air like smoke.

"We invite the Pale Cities delegation to examine this evidence. We welcome technical analysis from your engineers. We ask only for an honest engagement with the facts before us." He paused, meeting Councillor Vane's eyes directly. "And we ask for an explanation."

The silence that followed was absolute. Chogan could feel it pressing against his skin, could feel the tension radiating from both delegations. Beside him, Elder Blackriver sat with her hands folded, her expression unreadable. Behind him, he knew Aiyana was watching Keeper Drax's face, looking for the reaction that would confirm what they both suspected.

Councillor Vane cleared his throat. "Elder Grayfeather, on behalf of the Pale Cities, I want to express our deepest condolences for the loss of life at Tower Seven. Whatever the cause of this tragedy, we share your grief at its human cost."

It was the correct response. The diplomatic response. Chogan acknowledged it with a slight nod, knowing that what came next would matter far more than expressions of sympathy.

"However," Vane continued, "I must note that the evidence you have presented, while certainly troubling, does not conclusively establish the origin of the disruption signal. External interference could come from many sources. Natural phenomena we don't yet understand. Rogue actors operating outside governmental control. Even, with respect, internal sabotage designed to create a pretext for conflict."

The last suggestion was an insult wrapped in diplomatic language. Chogan felt Elder Blackriver stiffen beside him, felt Commander Speaks-Low's hand move slightly toward the ceremonial blade at his hip. He raised his own hand, a subtle gesture of restraint.

"Councillor Vane," he said quietly, "we have not accused the Pale Cities of responsibility for this attack. We have presented evidence and asked for dialogue. If your position is that the evidence is inconclusive, we are prepared to discuss what additional information might resolve that uncertainty."

"Our position," Keeper Drax interjected, her voice cutting through the exchange like a blade, "is that the Many Nations Alliance has a documented history of technological instability. Before we entertain accusations of external interference, perhaps we should examine whether this tragedy might have internal causes that your delegation finds politically inconvenient to acknowledge."

Chogan turned to face her. Her expression remained perfectly neutral, but he could see something moving behind her eyes. Not guilt. Not fear. Something closer to anticipation.

She had been waiting for this moment. Had prepared for it. Had, perhaps, helped to create it.

"Keeper Drax," he said, "the Many Nations Alliance welcomes scrutiny of our technological record. We have nothing to hide."

"Then you will not object to a historical review." She smiled, thin and precise. "I have prepared a presentation examining documented instances of Wind Spine system failures over the past century. I believe the pattern will prove illuminating."

She did not wait for permission. Her hand moved to the display controls, replacing Chogan's harmonic data with her own carefully curated images. Documents. Technical reports. A narrative of failure and instability, constructed from fragments of truth and careful omissions.

Chogan watched it unfold, recognizing the technique. Every piece of evidence she presented was technically accurate. Every citation was properly formatted. And every conclusion was a lie, built from truths arranged to deceive.

This was what Keeper Drax did. This was what she had spent her career perfecting. She did not fabricate. She *shaped*. And shaping, he knew, was far more dangerous than simple lies, because it was so much harder to refute.

* * *

The presentation lasted forty-five minutes.

Drax spoke with the calm authority of absolute certainty, walking the chamber through three alleged incidents of Wind Spine failure. The first, she claimed, had occurred sixty years ago in the northern territories, when a tower had collapsed during a winter storm. The second, thirty years past, had involved a resonance cascade that damaged several connected nodes. The third, barely a decade old, had resulted in temporary blackouts across a significant portion of the network.

Chogan knew the truth behind each incident. The first had been caused by an earthquake, not system failure. The second had been the result of deliberate Pale City sabotage, documented in MNA archives that Drax had clearly not consulted.

The third had been a controlled shutdown during a maintenance cycle, exaggerated beyond recognition.

But correcting her would require revealing classified information. Would require admitting that the MNA had evidence of previous Pale City attacks that it had chosen, for diplomatic reasons, not to publicize. Would require, in short, exactly the kind of escalation that the Pale Cities seemed to be hoping for.

So he sat, and listened, and let her weave her careful web of half-truths.

"In conclusion," Drax said, her voice carrying the weight of manufactured regret, "while the Many Nations Alliance has achieved remarkable technological advances, their organic approach to infrastructure carries inherent risks. Biological systems fail. Living structures decay. The tragedy at Tower Seven, however terrible, fits a pattern of vulnerability that the MNA has consistently refused to acknowledge."

She returned to her seat, her expression one of somber concern. Councillor Vane nodded slowly, as if hearing difficult truths for the first time. The junior delegates scribbled notes on their tablets.

And behind Chogan, he heard Aiyana draw a sharp breath.

He turned slightly, just enough to catch her eye. Her face was pale, her hands gripping the arms of her chair with white-knuckled intensity. She had heard something in Drax's presentation. Had recognized something wrong. He could see the realization moving through her, the anger building behind her careful composure.

He gave her the smallest shake of his head.

Not now. Not here.

She understood. He could see that too. She settled back in her chair, her expression hardening into something that would serve her well in the days ahead.

"The Many Nations Alliance thanks Keeper Drax for her thorough historical analysis," Chogan said, rising again. His voice was steady, betraying none of the cold fury building in his chest. "We will review the documentation she has provided and respond in tomorrow's session."

It was a tactical retreat, and everyone in the room knew it. But it was also a promise. The MNA would respond. And when they did, they would have more than righteous anger on their side.

"This session is adjourned," the administrator announced. "Delegations will reconvene tomorrow at nine hundred hours."

The chamber began to empty, delegates rising, conversations beginning in hushed tones. Chogan remained standing, watching the Pale Cities representatives gather their materials. Keeper Drax caught his eye one final time, and in that moment, the mask slipped. Just for an instant. Just long enough for him to see the satisfaction beneath.

She thought she had won the day. And perhaps she had. But wars were not won in single days, and Chogan Grayfeather had been fighting this one for thirty years.

He would not stop now.

* * *

That evening, Chogan walked the grounds of Threshold alone.

The gardens were quiet in the fading light, the hybrid architecture casting long shadows across pathways that seemed to have grown rather than been laid. He had always found this place melancholy. A reminder of what might have been, if his ancestors and theirs had found a way to coexist. If fear had not won out over hope.

Elder Blackriver found him near the central fountain, where

water flowed through channels shaped by both MNA cultivation and Pale City engineering. She moved quietly for a woman of her years, settling onto a bench beside him without speaking.

They sat in silence for a while, listening to the water, watching the stars emerge in a sky untouched by artificial light.

"You did not fail," she said finally. "The failure was decided before we arrived."

"I know." Chogan's voice was heavy with exhaustion. "Drax had her presentation prepared before Tower Seven fell. Perhaps before the attack was even launched. They were ready for us."

"And yet you chose to present our evidence anyway."

"It needed to be on record. For history, if nothing else." He paused. "And I needed to see their faces when they heard it. To know if any of them understood what they had done."

"Did you see what you hoped to see?"

Chogan thought of Councillor Vane, his exhausted eyes and careful words. Thought of Keeper Drax, her mask slipping for just a moment. Thought of the young man in the observer seats, the junior attaché who had watched everything with an expression of growing unease.

"I saw guilt," he said. "And I saw denial. And I saw at least one person who is beginning to question what he has been taught." He turned to meet Blackriver's eyes. "That may have to be enough."

"It is not enough."

"No. But it is a beginning."

Blackriver was silent for a moment. Then: "The young engineer. Aiyana. She recognized something in Drax's presentation."

"Yes. The citations were fabricated. At least some of them. Aiyana has spent years studying our technological history. She knows the real records."

"And you stopped her from speaking."

"I stopped her from speaking *today.* There will be a better time. A moment when the truth will do more than simply embarrass our opponents." Chogan's hands tightened on the edge of the bench. "Drax is clever. If we challenge her citations publicly, she will have explanations ready. Archive discrepancies. Classification protocols. Plausible deniability for every lie she told. We need more than righteous anger. We need proof that cannot be explained away."

"And if such proof does not exist?"

"Then we will have to create the conditions under which the truth reveals itself." Chogan rose, suddenly restless. "The Pale Cities are not monolithic, Winona. There are factions. Dissent. People who suspect what their government has done and want no part of it. If we can reach them, if we can provide them with evidence they cannot ignore, we may be able to prevent the war that Drax and her allies are trying to start."

"That is a dangerous game."

"All games worth playing are dangerous." He looked up at the stars, at the cold light of suns that had burned for millions of years and would burn for millions more, indifferent to the small dramas unfolding beneath them. "Our task now is to ensure that this failure does not become permanent. To buy time for reason to prevail."

"And if reason does not prevail?"

Chogan did not answer. He did not have an answer. He had only the work, the endless work of diplomacy, the small daily effort to hold back a tide that seemed determined to sweep them all away.

Tomorrow, the summit would continue. Tomorrow, he would sit across from people who had killed fourteen of his people and listen to them explain why it was the MNA's own fault. Tomorrow, he would maintain his composure, speak his careful words, play the game that might be the only thing standing between two civilizations and annihilation.

Tonight, he stood in a garden that had been built by people who believed in cooperation, and he mourned for the world they had imagined and never quite achieved.

The fountain murmured beside him, water flowing through channels shaped by two traditions, two philosophies, two peoples who had once believed they could build something beautiful together.

He wondered if they had been fools.

He wondered if he was a fool for still believing what they had believed.

He did not have answers. He had only tomorrow, and the work, and the small stubborn flame of hope that thirty years of disappointment had not quite extinguished.

It would have to be enough.

8

What the Archives Hold

Elias could not stop thinking about the citations.

He lay awake through most of the night, staring at the unfamiliar ceiling of his Threshold quarters, his mind circling back again and again to what he had found. Documents that didn't exist. Records that had been modified. A presentation built on foundations that crumbled under the slightest scrutiny.

By morning, he had convinced himself that there must be an explanation. Archive systems were complex. Access levels varied. Perhaps the documents existed in classified sections he couldn't reach. Perhaps the modifications he had seen were corrections to earlier errors, not falsifications. Perhaps Keeper Drax, for all her coldness, was simply working with incomplete information.

Perhaps. But the word rang hollow even in his own thoughts.

He attended the morning session in a fog, taking notes he would not remember writing, watching the delegations spar over procedural matters that suddenly seemed insignificant. The MNA had requested a joint technical review of the Tower Seven data. The Pale Cities had countered with demands for access to MNA network architecture. Back and forth, point and counterpoint, while fourteen people remained dead and no one spoke their names.

He watched Keeper Drax throughout. Tried to see past the mask of professional competence to whatever lay beneath. But she gave nothing away. Her responses were measured, her objections reasonable, her entire demeanor that of someone engaged in legitimate disagreement rather than active deception.

Either she was innocent, or she was the most accomplished liar Elias had ever encountered.

Neither possibility brought him comfort.

* * *

The break came at midday, both delegations retreating to their respective quarters for rest and consultation. Elias should have joined them. Should have reported to Keeper Drax for his afternoon assignments, reviewed the documentation protocols, prepared for tomorrow's sessions.

Instead, he found himself walking toward the gardens.

Threshold's grounds were extensive, sprawling across several acres of carefully maintained wilderness. The paths wound through groves of trees that seemed to have been encouraged rather than planted, past streams that followed natural courses rather than engineered channels, under skies unmarked by the atmospheric processors that defined Nova-Providence's horizon. It was beautiful in a way that made Elias's chest ache.

He walked without direction, letting his feet choose the path while his mind wrestled with questions that had no good answers. He was so absorbed in his thoughts that he almost didn't notice the figure sitting on a bench at the path's curve, until he was nearly upon her.

75

The young woman from the MNA delegation. The one with the angry eyes.

She looked up as he approached, her expression shifting from distant grief to guarded attention. An eagle perched on the bench beside her, its golden feathers catching the filtered sunlight, its gaze fixed on Elias with an intensity that made him want to step backward.

"I'm sorry," he said, stopping at what he hoped was a respectful distance. "I didn't mean to intrude."

She studied him for a long moment. Her eyes were dark, still rimmed with the shadows of sleepless nights, but there was something sharp beneath the exhaustion. An assessment being made. A judgment being formed.

"You're one of them," she said. Not accusation, exactly. More like observation. "The Pale Cities delegation."

"Junior cultural attaché." The title felt inadequate. Absurd, even. "Elias Harren."

"Aiyana Waketah." She did not offer her hand. Did not smile. But she did not tell him to leave. "You were watching yesterday. During Drax's presentation."

"It's my job. To observe. To document."

"Is that all you do? Observe and document?" There was an edge to the question. A challenge hidden beneath the simple words.

Elias hesitated. He should walk away. Should return to his quarters, prepare his reports, forget this conversation ever happened. He was not supposed to engage with the MNA delegation outside of official channels. It was a violation of protocol at best, potential grounds for dismissal at worst.

But the questions wouldn't stop. And something in her eyes suggested that she might have answers.

"May I sit?" he asked.

She considered him for another long moment. Then she nodded, a slight movement that seemed to cost her something. The eagle shifted on its perch, making room, its fierce eyes never leaving Elias's face.

He sat at the far end of the bench, leaving as much space between them as possible. The silence stretched, filled by the rustle of leaves and the distant murmur of water.

"You were there," he said finally. "At Tower Seven. When it fell."

Her face tightened. "Yes."

"I'm sorry." The words felt pathetically inadequate. "For your loss. For all of it."

"Are you?" She turned to look at him directly, and he felt the weight of her attention like a physical force. "Or are you sorry that it's making your delegation's job more difficult?"

"Both," he admitted. "But the first more than the second."

Something flickered in her expression. Surprise, perhaps. Or the beginning of something that wasn't quite contempt.

"You're honest," she said. "That's unexpected."

"Is it?"

"Your Keeper Drax spent forty-five minutes yesterday lying to our faces with perfect composure. I assumed it was a cultural trait."

The accusation hit like a blow. Elias felt his face flush, felt the instinctive denial rising in his throat.

She wasn't lying. She was presenting evidence. You're the ones who are distorting the truth.

But he didn't say it. Couldn't say it. Because he had seen the modified documents. Had traced the citations that led nowhere. Had spent the night wrestling with implications he was only beginning to understand.

"I noticed something," he said instead. Slowly. Carefully. As if testing ice that might not hold his weight. "In her presentation. Some of the citations didn't match our archives. I thought it might be an error, but..."

He trailed off. Aiyana was watching him with sudden intensity, her exhaustion momentarily forgotten.

"But what?"

"One of the documents was modified. Three days before the summit. The original version said something different than what Drax presented." He swallowed. "Something very different."

Aiyana was very still. Beside her, the eagle had gone motionless, its predator's attention fixed entirely on Elias.

"Why are you telling me this?"

It was a good question. He wasn't sure he had a good answer.

"Because I don't know what it means," he said finally. "And I don't know who I can ask. Everyone in my delegation either already knows what Drax is doing, or they're like me, observing and documenting without understanding what we're actually seeing." He met her eyes. "You were there. You saw what happened to your tower. You know things I don't. I thought maybe..."

"Maybe I could tell you whether your suspicions are justified?"

"Yes."

She was quiet for a long moment. The garden sounds seemed louder in the silence: birdsong, water, wind through leaves. A world that didn't care about summits or politics or the lies people told each other.

"The tower didn't fail," she said. Her voice was flat, controlled, but Elias could hear the emotion beneath. "It was attacked. An external signal, designed to disrupt our harmonic systems. Our engineers couldn't counter it because it was adaptive. It learned our responses and adjusted to defeat them."

"That's... that's what Elder Grayfeather said in the session. But he didn't present evidence of where the signal came from."

"Because we don't have direct proof. Not the kind that would satisfy your delegation's demands for certainty." Her jaw tightened. "But we know the signal wasn't natural. We know it used technology that our society doesn't develop because it's antithetical to our values. And we know that your Keeper Drax arrived at this summit with a presentation designed to blame us for our own destruction, complete with fabricated citations you've apparently already discovered."

"That doesn't prove the Pale Cities did it."

"No." Her voice was bitter. "It just proves that someone wanted it to happen and was ready to exploit it before the bodies were cold."

Elias looked away, unable to hold her gaze. The garden blurred before him, colors running together like watercolors in rain.

"I don't know what to do," he admitted. "I'm a junior attaché. I have no power, no influence. If I report what I found, it will be explained away or classified or I'll simply be removed from the delegation for overstepping my role."

"Then why tell me? Why take the risk?"

He thought about it. Really thought about it, for the first time since he had sat down.

"Because my father died in the Frontier," he said slowly. "When I was sixteen. He was an engineer, part of a survey team mapping resource deposits near the border. It was classified as equipment failure, but there were always rumors. Questions that never got answered."

The memory surfaced unbidden: his father's workshop, late at night, the two of them bent over schematics while his mother slept. His father had been designing a water purification system, something that could work without the massive infrastructure the Pale Cities usually required. *"Smaller scale,"* he'd said, his eyes bright with possibility. *"Distributed. Something that could help people in the outer settlements, maybe even across the border. Technology should serve everyone, Elias. Not just those who can afford it."*

Two months later, he was dead. The designs had vanished with him, classified or destroyed, Elias never learned which.

"I spent years telling myself the rumors were wrong," he continued. "That our government wouldn't lie about something like that. That there had to be a good reason for the secrecy." He paused. "I'm starting to think I was wrong. About all of it."

"What do you want?" Aiyana asked. "If you could change things. Not just expose lies, but actually build something different. What would it look like?"

The question caught him off guard. No one had ever asked him that before. In Nova-Providence, you didn't talk about changing things. You talked about preserving them, protecting them, defending the way things were against the chaos outside.

"Something honest," he said finally. "A society that doesn't need lies to hold itself together. Where people can ask questions without being afraid of the answers." He gestured at the garden around them, at the trees that grew without being forced into shapes. "Maybe something more like this. Where things are allowed to find their own form instead of being controlled into submission."

It was more than he had ever admitted to anyone, including himself. But sitting here, in this impossible garden between two worlds, it felt like the truest thing he had ever said.

Aiyana's expression shifted. Something softer entering the grief and anger. Not sympathy, exactly. More like recognition.

"My brother is in the Frontier," she said quietly. "Somewhere. I don't know where exactly. He went to help people, to build bridges between our societies. I haven't heard from him in months." She reached out and touched the eagle's feathers, a gesture that seemed unconscious. "I came to this summit hoping to find information about him. Instead, I watched the people who probably killed my colleagues lie to my face about it."

"I'm sorry," Elias said again. It was still inadequate. But it was all he had.

"So am I." She rose from the bench, the eagle shifting to her shoulder with practiced ease. "I should go. My delegation will wonder where I am."

"Will you tell them? About what I said?"

She considered the question. "I'll tell Elder Grayfeather. He should know that someone in your delegation has doubts. Beyond that..." She shrugged. "It's your information. Your risk. You decide what to do with it."

She turned to go, then paused, looking back at him over her shoulder.

"Elias Harren." His name sounded strange in her accent, the syllables shaped differently than he was used to hearing. "If you find more, if you learn something that matters, there are ways to reach me. Threshold has communication channels that aren't monitored by either delegation. Ask the staff about the old observatory network."

Then she was gone, disappearing around a curve in the path, leaving Elias alone with the garden and his thoughts and the slowly settling realization of what he had just done.

He had shared classified concerns with a member of an opposing delegation. He had expressed doubt about his own government's honesty. He had, in the language of the protocols he had memorized, potentially compromised the security of Pale Cities diplomatic operations.

He should feel guilty. Should feel afraid. Should be racing back to his quarters to file a report admitting his indiscretion before someone else discovered it.

Instead, he felt lighter than he had since arriving at Threshold. As if a weight he hadn't known he was carrying had been set down, at least for a moment.

The truth was still out there, hidden in archives and classified reports and the careful silences of people who knew more than they were saying. But for the first time, Elias felt like he might be moving toward it rather than away.

He pulled his father's compass from his pocket and held it in his palm. The needle pointed east, as it always did. Toward home. Toward everything he had been taught to believe.

But the needle didn't know what he knew now. Didn't know about modified documents and fabricated citations and a Keeper who had arrived at the summit with lies already prepared. The compass pointed to Nova-Providence. But Nova-Providence wasn't the home he had always believed it to be.

He closed his fist around the compass and walked back toward the residence halls, leaving the garden behind.

There was more to find. He was certain of that now.

And he was going to find it, whatever the cost.

9

The View from Command

Captain Lucian Ford had learned, over fifteen years of military service, to trust his instincts.

They had saved his life in the border skirmishes of his youth, when a moment's hesitation could mean the difference between returning home and being shipped back in a sealed container. They had guided him through the political minefields of officer promotion, teaching him when to speak and when to stay silent, when to follow orders and when to interpret them creatively. They had kept him alive, kept him advancing, kept him useful to people who valued usefulness above almost everything else.

Right now, his instincts were screaming.

He stood on the eastern terrace of Threshold's main building, running his dawn security check with the methodical precision that had become second nature. Perimeter sensors: functional. Sight lines: clear. Personnel positions: as assigned. The MNA delegation's quarters were visible across the courtyard, their organic architecture catching the first light in ways that made his tactical mind itch with discomfort. Too many blind spots. Too many places where threats could hide.

But the threats he was worried about weren't hiding in the MNA's curved walls and living surfaces. They were sitting in his own delegation's conference rooms, wearing gray uniforms and speaking in carefully modulated tones about historical precedent and technological vulnerability.

Keeper Drax's presentation yesterday had been masterful. He could acknowledge that even as it made his skin crawl. Every point perfectly supported. Every citation precisely formatted. Every conclusion drawing inexorably toward the narrative she wanted to establish: that the MNA's tragedy was their own fault, a consequence of inherent weaknesses in their approach to technology.

Lucian had seen enough propaganda in his career to recognize it when it was being deployed. What troubled him was that he couldn't quite identify the lie. Everything Drax had said was technically accurate, as far as he could verify. The documents existed. The incidents had occurred. The pattern she described was at least plausible.

And yet.

He had watched her face when news of the tower collapse arrived. Had seen the flash of something that wasn't surprise. Had noted how quickly she pivoted from condolence to narrative control, as if she had been waiting for exactly this opportunity.

Coincidence, perhaps. Preparation for multiple contingencies, as any good strategist would maintain. But Lucian's instincts said otherwise. His instincts said that Keeper Drax had known something was coming. Had perhaps helped it come.

He had no proof. He had only the cold certainty in his gut, the same certainty that had kept him alive through situations where proof was a luxury no one could afford.

* * *

The MNA security commander found him there an hour later.

Lucian heard the footsteps approaching, recognized their rhythm as trained and deliberate, and did not turn around. He had been expecting this meeting, or something like it. Professional courtesy demanded an exchange between security leads. Protocol required at least a minimal coordination of protective measures. What neither protocol nor courtesy required was the conversation that would actually take place.

"Captain Ford." The voice was deep, measured, carrying the careful neutrality of someone who had spent years choosing his words with precision. "I am Commander Talon Speaks-Low. I oversee security for the Alliance delegation."

Lucian turned. The man before him was tall, broad-shouldered, with the kind of weathered features that spoke of years spent in harsh conditions. His eyes were dark and watchful, assessing Lucian with the same professional attention that Lucian was directing at him. Two predators, recognizing each other across the artificial boundary of opposing delegations.

"Commander." Lucian inclined his head slightly. "I've read your file. Impressive service record."

"As is yours." A faint smile touched the corner of Speaks-Low's mouth. "The Brennan Ridge incident. Forty-eight hours holding a position against superior numbers. Your superiors must have been pleased."

"My superiors were pleased that I didn't die and create a diplomatic incident. The holding action was secondary."

"Isn't it always." Speaks-Low moved to stand beside him at the terrace railing, looking out over the courtyard with an expression that revealed nothing. "This is a beautiful place.

Built by people who believed in something."

"And maintained by people who've forgotten what that something was."

The words came out before Lucian could stop them. He felt a flash of irritation at himself. He was not usually so unguarded. Something about this place, this situation, was wearing at his defenses.

Speaks-Low turned to look at him, surprise flickering briefly across his controlled features. "That's an unusual sentiment for a Pale Cities officer."

"It's an unusual summit."

They stood in silence for a moment, two men trained to kill each other finding themselves temporarily united by the strangeness of their circumstances. Below them, the court-yard was beginning to stir: staff members moving between buildings, delegates emerging for morning walks, the slow machinery of diplomacy grinding into motion.

"I knew some of the people who died at Tower Seven," Speaks-Low said quietly. "Not well. But I knew them. Good people. Engineers who spent their lives maintaining systems that kept thousands of others safe."

Lucian said nothing. There was nothing to say.

"Your delegation's position is that it was an accident. Internal failure. The price of our technological choices." Speaks-Low's voice remained level, but Lucian could hear the current of anger beneath. "You understand why we find that difficult to accept."

"I understand."

"Do you also understand that fourteen people are dead, and someone is responsible, and that responsibility does not disappear simply because it is inconvenient to acknowledge?"

Lucian turned to face him fully. "Commander, I'm a soldier. I follow orders. I protect the people I'm assigned to protect. I don't make policy, and I don't conduct investigations into matters above my clearance level."

"But you have eyes. And instincts. And enough experience to recognize when something doesn't add up."

It was a challenge, carefully phrased. An invitation to say something that could never be unsaid. Lucian felt the weight of it, felt the moment stretching between them like a wire pulled taut.

"I have eyes," he admitted finally. "And instincts. And they're telling me things I can't act on without proof. Without something more than suspicion."

Speaks-Low nodded slowly, as if this was the answer he had expected. "Proof is difficult when those who might have it are invested in ensuring it never comes to light."

"Yes."

"And yet proof has a way of emerging. Documents are copied. Witnesses remember. Systems record what their creators would prefer to forget." He paused. "I have been in your position, Captain. Knowing something is wrong, unable to prove it, uncertain whether proof would matter even if it existed. It is not a comfortable place to stand."

"No. It isn't."

"I will not ask you to betray your duty or your people. But I will ask you to remember something." Speaks-Low's eyes held his, dark and steady. "The people who died at Tower Seven were not your enemies. They were engineers and technicians, doing their jobs, maintaining systems that harmed no one. Whatever happens at this summit, whatever decisions are made in the rooms where we are not invited, those deaths deserve better than to become footnotes in someone else's strategy."

He turned and walked away, his footsteps fading into the morning quiet. Lucian watched him go, feeling the weight of the conversation settle into his chest like a stone dropped into deep water.

He had not agreed to anything. Had not promised anything. Had not crossed any of the lines that duty and protocol had drawn around his actions.

But something had shifted nonetheless. A door had been opened. A possibility acknowledged.

The sun was fully up now, burning away the morning mist, casting the courtyard in colors that seemed too bright for the darkness gathering at the edges of everything.

* * *

Keeper Drax summoned him that afternoon.

Her quarters were immaculate, every surface arranged with the same precision she brought to her presentations. She sat behind a small desk, documents spread before her, and did not rise when Lucian entered. The slight was deliberate, he knew. A reminder of hierarchies. Of who gave orders and who followed them.

"Captain Ford. Thank you for coming."

"Keeper." He remained standing, hands clasped behind his back in the posture of formal attention. "How may I assist you?"

"I require a security assessment." She did not look up from her documents. "The MNA delegation's movements, their communication patterns, their interactions with Threshold staff. I want to know everything they do when they are not in formal sessions."

It was a reasonable request. Monitoring opposing delegations was standard procedure at any diplomatic summit. And yet something in the way she phrased it made Lucian uneasy.

"I've already established surveillance protocols," he said carefully. "My team is tracking all significant movements and documenting any unusual patterns."

"I want more than tracking." Now she looked up, her eyes meeting his with the cool assessment of someone cataloging a tool's utility. "I want to know who they talk to. What they talk about. Whether any of them are meeting with anyone outside official channels."

"That would require resources beyond my current allocation. Audio surveillance in neutral territory is a protocol violation that could compromise our entire diplomatic position if discovered."

"Let me worry about diplomatic positions." Her voice sharpened slightly. "Your concern is security. And security requires information."

Lucian considered his response carefully. He was not naive enough to believe that Drax's interest in the MNA delegation was purely defensive. She was looking for something. Or looking to confirm something she already suspected.

"Is there a specific threat I should be aware of?" he asked. "Something that would justify enhanced surveillance measures?"

"The threat is the summit itself." Drax set down her pen and gave him her full attention. "The MNA came here with an agenda. They intend to use the Tower Seven incident to paint us as aggressors, to justify increased militarization of the border zones, to position themselves as victims requiring international sympathy. We cannot allow that narrative to take hold."

"With respect, Keeper, narrative control is your department. Mine is keeping our delegation safe."

"They are the same thing." She rose from her desk, moving around it to stand closer to him. She was small, barely reaching his shoulder, but there was nothing diminished about her presence. "The MNA will be looking for weaknesses in our position. Contradictions they can exploit. People in our delegation who might be persuaded to share information they shouldn't share." Her eyes narrowed slightly. "I need to know if any such vulnerabilities exist. And I need to know before they can be exploited."

Lucian felt his jaw tighten. She was asking him to spy on his own people. To report on the private conversations and potential doubts of Pale Cities citizens. It was technically within his authority. It was also deeply troubling.

"I will enhance surveillance on the MNA delegation within protocol limits," he said, keeping his voice neutral. "If I observe any concerning interactions with our personnel, I will report them through appropriate channels."

Drax studied him for a long moment. Whatever she was looking for, she apparently didn't find it, because her expression shifted from assessment to something closer to dismissal.

"That will have to do. For now." She returned to her desk. "You may go, Captain. I trust you will keep me informed of any developments."

"Of course, Keeper."

He left her quarters feeling as if he had just navigated a minefield in the dark. She hadn't trusted him with whatever she was really planning. That much was clear. She had probed for his loyalty, tested his willingness to bend the rules, and found him insufficiently pliable.

It should have been insulting. Instead, it was clarifying.

Keeper Drax was running an operation within the operation. Using the summit as cover for something she didn't want even her own security chief to know about. And whatever that something was, she was worried enough about exposure to start looking for leaks before any had actually occurred.

The instincts that had kept Lucian alive for fifteen years were screaming louder than ever.

* * *

That evening, Lucian walked the perimeter of Threshold's grounds alone.

It was part of his routine, the final check before night security protocols took over. But tonight, his attention was not on sensor placements or sight lines. Tonight, his mind was churning through everything he had seen and heard since arriving at this strange place between worlds.

He thought of Keeper Drax, her certainty and her secrets. Of Councillor Vane, his genuine distress and his political impotence. Of Commander Speaks-Low, asking him to remember that the dead deserved better than strategy. Of the young cultural attaché, Harren, whose face had gone pale during Drax's presentation, whose eyes had flickered with something that looked very much like doubt.

He thought of his daughter, back in Nova-Providence, eight years old and full of questions he didn't know how to answer. What kind of world was he building for her? What kind of future was he helping to create, following orders he didn't understand for people he didn't trust?

The sunset painted the sky in shades of amber and rose, colors that seemed impossible after a lifetime under Nova-Providence's calibrated light. Lucian stopped at the western edge of the grounds, where the cultivated gardens gave way to the wild growth of the Frontier, and watched the light fade into darkness.

Somewhere out there, beyond the boundary markers, the world went on without the careful management of either civilization. Animals hunted and were hunted. Plants grew and died according to rhythms no one controlled. Weather moved across the land without consultation with atmospheric processors or harmonic systems.

It should have seemed chaotic. Instead, it seemed peaceful. A reminder that there were ways of existing that neither the Pale Cities nor the MNA had invented.

Lucian did not believe in signs. Did not trust the universe to send messages to those who needed them. But standing there, watching the darkness spread across a land that belonged to no one, he felt something shift in his understanding.

He was a soldier. His duty was to follow orders, protect his people, serve the institutions that had given his life structure and meaning. But duty was not the same as blindness. And service did not require complicity in things that violated the principles that service was supposed to protect.

He would do his job. Would maintain security, run his patrols, file his reports. But he would also watch. Would pay attention to the things Keeper Drax didn't want him to notice. Would wait for the moment when watching became insufficient and action became necessary.

He did not know when that moment would come. Did not know what form it would take. But he knew, with the certainty of instincts honed over fifteen years of survival, that it
would come.

And when it did, he would be ready.

The last light faded from the sky. The stars emerged, cold and distant and utterly indifferent to the small dramas unfolding beneath them. Lucian turned and walked back toward the residence halls, his footsteps steady on the path, his mind already preparing for whatever tomorrow would bring.

Behind him, the Frontier waited in darkness. Patient. Unchanging. A reminder that some things endured no matter what walls were built to contain them.

Truth was one of those things.

It had a way of getting out.

10

Day Three

The drone appeared at midday.

Aiyana was walking the Threshold gardens, trying to clear her mind of another morning wasted on procedural objections. Four hours of delays while fourteen families still waited for answers. Sitala circled overhead, restless, sharing her frustration through the bond.

The eagle's cry cut through her thoughts. Aiyana looked up and saw it: an angular shape moving against the clouds, too regular to be a bird. A Pale Cities reconnaissance drone, well inside MNA airspace, moving with the confidence of a device that knew exactly where it was.

Through the bond, Sitala's impulse flared: *Intruder. Strike. Destroy.*

No, Aiyana thought back, though part of her wanted to let Sitala fly. *Wait. Watch.*

She ran toward the MNA residence hall. Commander Speaks-Low met her at the entrance, already flanked by two suited Sky Guardians.

"Reconnaissance configuration," he said. "It's here to provoke. If we shoot it down, they claim we attacked unprovoked. If we let it survey us, we look weak."

"Then let's stop playing their game." The words came out before Aiyana could stop them. "We have evidence of the tower attack. We have their drone in our airspace. Why are we still negotiating? Why aren't we doing something?"

Speaks-Low's eyes narrowed. "Because 'doing something' without a plan leads to war. And war is exactly what whoever sent that drone wants." He turned to the Guardians. "Harmonic pulse only. Bring it down intact."

The intercept took less than a minute. A precisely calibrated pulse disrupted the drone's systems. One Guardian caught it before it hit the ground, cradling the angular machine like a wounded bird.

Clean. Professional. Exactly what Speaks-Low had ordered.

And not nearly enough, Aiyana thought. Not when people were dying while diplomats talked in circles.

* * *

The emergency session that followed was a masterwork of diplomatic maneuvering.

Keeper Drax demanded an apology for the "attack" on Pale Cities equipment. Chogan countered by proposing a joint technical review of the drone's data storage. The suggestion caught Drax off guard; whatever advantage the incursion was meant to create had been neutralized.

Councillor Vane, looking exhausted, offered the compromise that let both sides step back: the Pale Cities acknowledged the drone had entered disputed airspace and agreed to review their protocols.

It wasn't justice. It wasn't even close. But it was enough to prevent escalation.

As the delegations filed out, Aiyana caught Drax's expression in an unguarded moment: cold, frustrated, recalculating. The drone incident had not gone as planned. But Aiyana felt no sense of victory. Only the certainty that whoever was orchestrating events would try again.

They would keep trying until they got what they wanted.

And what they wanted was war.

* * *

That evening, a message arrived through the old observatory network.

Found more. The third incident in Drax's presentation. It wasn't a failure. It was an attack. We attacked you. Thirty years ago. And then we erased it.

Aiyana read it three times. She had suspected as much. But suspicion was one thing. Confirmation was another.

She thought of Elias Harren, alone in his quarters, digging through archives that were supposed to support his government's position and finding instead evidence of its crimes. She should hate him. He was one of them, part of the system that had destroyed Tower Seven. His people had murdered fourteen engineers three days ago.

But she couldn't make herself feel the hatred. Not when she remembered his face in the garden, the confusion of someone whose world was crumbling. He was searching for truth. In a society built on lies, that made him something rare.

Something like her brother.

She composed her reply carefully: *Keep searching. We need proof that can't be denied. Be careful. They're watching everyone now.*

She had just conspired with a member of an opposing delegation. Violated every protocol. Placed her trust in someone who should be her enemy.

She didn't regret it.

Outside her window, Sitala perched on the designated roost, attention fixed on the eastern horizon. Through the bond, Aiyana felt what the eagle felt: the gathering pressure of a storm not yet visible.

"Kele," she whispered. "Where are you?"

She had spent years resenting him for leaving. For choosing his idealism over his family. For disappearing into the gray lands while she stayed behind to do practical work.

But now, exchanging secret messages with a Pale Cities attaché who was risking everything to find the truth, she understood something she hadn't before. Kele hadn't left because he didn't care. He had left because he cared too much. Because he couldn't accept a world divided by lies and fear.

She wasn't sure if that made him a hero or a fool. Maybe there wasn't as much difference between the two as she had always believed.

* * *

The note slipped under Chogan's door arrived shortly after midnight: a location and time in unremarkable handwriting. *Old observatory. North tower. 0200.*

He had a strong suspicion who had sent it. Only one member of the Pale Cities delegation had looked genuinely pained by the summit's deterioration. Only one had spoken of accommodation as if he actually believed in it.

Councillor Vane was waiting at the top of the north tower, silhouetted against stars that poured through the observatory's open dome.

"Thank you for coming," Vane said. "If Keeper Drax knew I was here, there would be consequences."

"Then why take the risk?"

Vane was silent for a long moment. "Because I have spent twenty years in politics. Twenty years of compromise and calculation. I have built a career on pragmatism." He paused. "But there are limits. There are things pragmatism cannot excuse."

"The tower."

"The tower." Vane's hands tightened on the railing. "I don't have proof. But I know, Elder. I know that what happened was not an accident. And I know this summit is being used to cover that crime rather than address it."

It was a remarkable admission. That Vane was willing to make it spoke to a desperation that went beyond political calculation.

"What do you hope to accomplish?" Chogan asked.

"A path that doesn't lead to open war. Some arrangement that gives both sides room to step back." Vane's voice cracked. "I have grandchildren, Elder. The youngest just turned two. I don't want them to grow up in a world at war because I was too proud to compromise."

Chogan closed his eyes. How many times had he stood in rooms like this, listening to men plead for compromise? How many times had that compromise simply delayed the reckoning?

"What are you proposing?"

They talked until the sky began to lighten. The proposal Vane outlined was carefully constructed: the MNA would accept "continuing investigation" of Tower Seven rather than definitive conclusions. In exchange, the Pale Cities would agree to a mutual monitoring arrangement along the border zones.

It was a trade: justice for transparency. The dead would not be avenged, but future deaths might be prevented.

"This is not justice," Chogan said finally. "But it may be enough to prevent the war that someone clearly wants to start. And that, for the moment, may have to be enough."

"How do we proceed?"

"I will draft language tonight. Present it at the morning session as an MNA proposal. You express surprise but willingness to consider. The appearance of spontaneity gives Drax less time to organize opposition."

"She'll know it wasn't spontaneous."

"She'll suspect. But by the time she has proof, the proposal will already be part of the official record." Chogan paused. "Harder to bury. Harder to pretend it never existed."

Vane extended his hand. "I hope we're not fools, Elder."

Chogan gripped it firmly. "Even if we are, the delay itself has value. Every day without war is a day when something might change. When the people who want destruction might lose their grip on power."

"That's a lot of hope to place in uncertainty."

"It's all the hope I have left."

Chogan worked through the remaining hours of darkness, crafting language with the care of a jeweler cutting diamonds. Every word mattered. Every phrase would be examined for hidden meanings.

By dawn, he had a draft he believed could work. Not perfect. Nothing was ever perfect in diplomacy. But workable. A foundation that could support something larger if both sides chose to build on it.

He washed his face, put on fresh robes, and prepared for the morning session.

For the first time since Tower Seven fell, he believed there might be a path forward. Even if it closed tomorrow, today it existed.

That was more than they had yesterday.

It would have to be enough.

11

The Leak

Elias was awake when the transmission went out.

He had been unable to sleep, his mind churning through everything he had learned, everything he had shared with Aiyana, everything that still remained hidden in archives he hadn't yet accessed. The hours before dawn had become his time for thinking, for staring at the ceiling and wondering how his life had become so complicated.

So he heard it. The soft chime of the communications terminal in the corridor outside his quarters. The murmur of voices, too quiet to make out words but too urgent to be routine. And then footsteps, quick and purposeful, moving toward Keeper Drax's rooms.

He rose and dressed quickly, some instinct telling him that whatever was happening, he needed to see it. Needed to understand. The corridor was empty when he emerged, but light spilled from under Drax's door, and he could hear the rapid clicking of keys, the hum of equipment being pushed beyond its normal operating parameters.

He didn't dare approach. Instead, he found a shadow near

the corridor's end and waited, watching, his heart pounding against his ribs.

Ten minutes passed. Fifteen. Then Drax's door opened, and she emerged, her face composed in an expression of grim satisfaction. She moved down the corridor without seeing him, her steps carrying her toward the communications center with the purpose of someone who had just set something irreversible in motion.

Elias waited until she was gone, then moved to her door. It was locked, of course. But the communications terminal in the corridor was still active, its screen glowing with the residue of recent transmissions.

He shouldn't look. He knew he shouldn't look. But his fingers were moving before his conscience could stop them, pulling up the transmission log, scanning the headers for anything that might explain what Drax had been doing at this hour.

Priority transmission. Nova-Providence. Signal Mesh Central Authority.

The content was encrypted, beyond his ability to access. But the header told him enough. Drax had just sent something directly to the people who controlled what every citizen of the Pale Cities saw and heard. Had bypassed normal diplomatic channels, normal authorization protocols, normal everything.

Whatever she had sent, it was meant to be seen before anyone could stop it.

Elias backed away from the terminal, his hands shaking. He didn't know what was coming. But he knew it was bad. Knew it with the same instinct that had kept him awake, that had driven him to search archives and question narratives and reach out to someone who should have been his enemy.

He returned to his quarters and waited for dawn, for the

morning session, for whatever catastrophe Keeper Drax had just unleashed.

He didn't have to wait long.

* * *

The Signal Mesh broadcast hit Nova-Providence at 0600 hours, timed to catch the morning information cycle.

Elias saw it on the delegation's internal feed, the same broadcast that would be playing on every screen in every home and workplace across the Pale Cities. The headline scrolled across the bottom of the display in urgent red letters:

BREAKING: MNA ADMITS TOWER FAILURE INCONCLUSIVE. DEMANDS UNPRECEDENTED ACCESS TO PALE CITIES TERRITORY.

The accompanying story was worse. It described a secret MNA proposal, leaked by anonymous sources, that would require the Pale Cities to open their border installations to foreign inspection. The framing was masterful: the MNA had failed to prove their accusations of sabotage and were now demanding compensation for their own failures. They wanted access to Pale Cities military positions. They wanted to compromise national security. They wanted surrender dressed up as diplomacy.

None of it was true. Or rather, all of it was true, but twisted beyond recognition. The proposal had called for *mutual* monitoring, access for both sides. It had been framed as a step toward transparency, not a demand for surrender. It had been the product of careful negotiation between people who genuinely wanted to prevent war.

And now it was poison. Transformed into exactly the kind of MNA overreach that would inflame public opinion and make any cooperation impossible.

Elias watched the broadcast with growing horror, understanding now what Drax had done. She had taken Councillor Vane's attempt at peace and turned it into a weapon. Had used the truth as raw material for a lie so effective that it would be believed by millions of people who would never know what had actually been proposed.

The delegation's common room filled rapidly as other members arrived, drawn by the broadcast, their faces showing varying degrees of shock and confusion. Councillor Vane appeared last, his complexion gray, his movements those of a man who had just watched something he loved being destroyed.

"Councillor." One of his advisors approached, tablet in hand. "The Assembly is demanding a statement. The public response is... significant."

"I can imagine." Vane's voice was hollow. He didn't look at anyone, his gaze fixed on the broadcast that continued to scroll its poisoned version of events across every screen in the room.

"Sir, if we could clarify the actual terms of the proposal..."

"What proposal?" Keeper Drax's voice cut through the room like a blade. She stood in the doorway, her expression one of careful concern. "I'm not aware of any formal proposal from the MNA delegation. Are you, Councillor?"

The silence that followed was suffocating. Elias watched Vane's face cycle through emotions: shock, then fury, then the terrible realization that he had been outmaneuvered. Whatever he said now would be measured against what Drax had already established as the official narrative. If he admitted to secret negotiations, he would be accused of exceeding his authority, of making unauthorized concessions, of betraying Pale Cities interests. If he denied them, he would be complicit in the lie.

Drax had trapped him perfectly. Had used his own attempt at peace to destroy any possibility of it.

"No," Vane said finally, the word coming out like a surrender. "No formal proposal. The broadcast must be based on... speculation. Misinterpretation of informal discussions."

"I see." Drax nodded, her expression one of sympathetic understanding. "Then we should issue a statement clarifying that. Making clear that the Pale Cities have made no commitments and accepted no terms that would compromise our security."

"Yes." The word was barely audible. "Yes, we should do that."

Elias turned away, unable to watch anymore. Unable to see the man who had tried to prevent war being forced to participate in its preparation. Unable to witness the precise, surgical destruction of hope.

He left the common room and walked blindly through Threshold's corridors, not knowing where he was going, only knowing that he needed to be somewhere else. Somewhere he couldn't hear the broadcasts. Somewhere he couldn't see the satisfaction in Keeper Drax's eyes.

Somewhere he could pretend, even for a moment, that this wasn't happening.

* * *

The final session of the summit began at noon.

There was nothing left to negotiate. Both sides knew it. The MNA delegation sat in rigid silence, their faces masks of controlled fury. The Pale Cities delegation maintained the fiction of diplomatic engagement, but the words they spoke were empty, formalities rendered meaningless by what had already been done.

Elias watched from his usual seat in the observers' section, his tablet open to a blank page. He was supposed to be documenting the session, recording the official proceedings for the Doctrine Halls. But there was nothing to record. Nothing real. Just the careful performance of people going through motions that no longer meant anything.

Chogan Grayfeather spoke first. His voice was steady, but Elias could see the cost of that steadiness in the set of his shoulders, the tightness around his eyes. He had spent thirty years building toward moments like this, and he had just watched his work destroyed in a single morning broadcast.

"The Many Nations Alliance came to this summit in good faith," he said. "We presented evidence of an attack on our people. We offered dialogue. We proposed measures that would build trust between our societies and reduce the risk of future conflict."

He paused, his gaze moving slowly across the Pale Cities delegation. When he continued, his voice had dropped, becoming something quieter and far more dangerous.

"Those proposals have been misrepresented. Our intentions have been distorted. The possibility of cooperation has been deliberately destroyed by those who prefer conflict to peace." Another pause. "We know who bears responsibility for this. We will not forget."

Keeper Drax rose to respond, her expression one of measured regret. "The Many Nations Alliance's disappointment is understandable. This summit has not produced the outcomes any of us hoped for. But we must be careful not to assign blame where none is warranted. The gap between our societies remains wide. Closing it will require time, patience, and mutual respect."

"Mutual respect." Elder Blackriver spoke for the first time, her voice sharp with contempt. "Is that what you call it when you leak private discussions to your propaganda networks? When you twist proposals into accusations? When you sabotage any possibility of progress before it can threaten your preferred narrative?"

"I don't know what you're referring to." Drax's smile was thin and utterly without warmth. "The broadcast this morning was based on information that became available through normal channels. If the MNA is unhappy with how their positions have been characterized, perhaps they should have been clearer in their communications."

The lie was so brazen, so perfectly delivered, that Elias felt something crack inside him. This was what Keeper Drax did. This was what the Doctrine Office existed to do. They took truth and twisted it, took hope and poisoned it, took any possibility of a better world and strangled it before it could breathe.

And he had been part of it. Had documented their lies. Had believed their narratives. Had spent his whole life accepting a version of history that was as carefully constructed as any of Drax's presentations.

He looked across the room and found Aiyana Waketah's eyes. She was watching him, her expression unreadable. But he saw the question there, the same question she had asked in the garden:

Do you know what your people did?

Yes, he thought. Yes, I know. I've always known, somewhere. I just didn't want to see it.

The session dragged on for another hour, but nothing more of substance was said. Positions were restated. Regrets were expressed. The language of diplomacy was deployed to paper over the reality that diplomacy had failed.

When it finally ended, the two delegations rose and faced each other across the chamber. No one spoke. No one moved to shake hands or exchange the customary closing pleasantries. They simply looked at each other, enemies acknowledging what they had always been, the pretense of negotiation finally stripped away.

Then the MNA delegation turned and walked out, and the summit was over.

* * *

Elias found Councillor Vane alone in the gardens that evening, sitting on a bench near the fountain, staring at nothing.

He shouldn't approach. It wasn't his place. But something drove him forward anyway, some need to acknowledge what had happened, to offer witness if nothing else.

"Councillor."

Vane looked up, his eyes red-rimmed and unfocused. For a moment, he seemed not to recognize Elias. Then something shifted in his expression, a weary acknowledgment of another human presence.

"Harren. The cultural attaché." His voice was flat. "Come to document my failure?"

"No, sir." Elias hesitated, then sat down on the bench, leaving a respectful distance between them. "I came to say I'm sorry. For what it's worth."

"It's not worth much." Vane laughed, a harsh sound without humor. "But thank you for saying it."

They sat in silence for a while, the fountain murmuring beside them. The gardens were empty, everyone else occupied with packing or preparations for departure. Tomorrow, they would all return to their separate worlds, and the brief fiction of neutral ground would end.

"I tried," Vane said finally, his voice barely above a whisper. "I actually believed we could accomplish something here. That if we could just talk, just listen to each other, we might find a way forward." He shook his head. "Naive. Drax warned me. Said the MNA would never negotiate in good faith. I thought she was being cynical."

"The MNA was negotiating in good faith." The words came out before Elias could stop them. "The proposal was real. The compromise was real. Someone on our side destroyed it."

Vane turned to look at him, his tired eyes sharpening. "What do you know about it?"

"I know that Keeper Drax sent a priority transmission to Nova-Providence early this morning. Before dawn. Before anyone else was awake." Elias kept his voice low, aware of the risk he was taking. "I know the broadcast that followed was perfectly timed to destroy any chance of the summit succeeding."

"You're accusing a Doctrine Keeper of sabotaging our own diplomatic mission."

"I'm telling you what I observed." Elias met his eyes steadily. "What you do with that information is your choice."

Vane was silent for a long moment. The implications hung between them, vast and terrible. If what Elias was suggesting was true, then the summit hadn't failed. It had been murdered. And the killer was sitting in their own delegation, wearing the gray uniform of the Doctrine Office, smiling her thin smile as she burned down any hope of peace.

"Why are you telling me this?" Vane asked finally.

"Because someone should know." Elias paused. "And because I've spent the last several days discovering things about our government that I can't unknow. Modified archives. Fabricated citations. A pattern of deception that goes back decades." He looked away, unable to hold Vane's gaze. "I don't know what to do with it. I don't have the power to change anything. But you do. Or you might."

"Power." Vane laughed again, bitterly. "I just watched everything I've built get destroyed in a single morning. Whatever power I had, Drax has made clear how easily it can be taken away."

"Then we have nothing to lose." Elias rose from the bench. "I'm going to keep looking. Keep searching. Whatever I find, I'll make sure it reaches people who might use it." He paused. "You can pretend this conversation never happened. Go back to Nova-Providence, salvage what's left of your career, tell yourself there was nothing you could have done."

"Or?"

"Or you can remember what you felt last night, when you thought peace was possible. And you can help me prove that the people who took it away don't deserve to define our future."

He walked away before Vane could respond, his heart pounding, his hands shaking. He had just revealed himself to someone who could destroy him with a word. Had trusted a man he barely knew with information that could end his career, his freedom, possibly his life.

But he couldn't stay silent anymore. Couldn't watch the truth be buried and say nothing. Couldn't pretend that the lies he had been taught were acceptable simply because they were familiar.

Behind him, Councillor Vane remained on the bench, staring at the fountain, his face unreadable.

The water flowed on, indifferent to the small human dramas unfolding around it. Indifferent to summits and betrayals, to lies and the truth that struggled against them.

Tomorrow, they would all go home. And the Cold War would begin in earnest.

But tonight, in a garden built by people who had believed in cooperation, a seed had been planted. Small. Fragile. Easily destroyed.

But alive.

12

The Borders Harden

Aiyana returned to a world that had changed while she was gone.

The flight back from Threshold took her over landscapes she had known her entire life, but they looked different now. The forests seemed darker, the rivers narrower, the spaces between settlements more vast and empty. She watched through the sky-craft's window as the familiar geography of home unfolded beneath her, and felt like a stranger seeing it for the first time.

Beside her, Sitala rode in her traveling perch, her golden feathers ruffled from the journey. Through the bond, Aiyana felt the eagle's unease, a reflection of her own turbulent emotions. They had left the MNA as representatives of a society that still believed in peace. They were returning to one that was preparing for war.

The signs were everywhere. Sky Guardian patrols that had once been ceremonial now flew in combat formations. Communications towers bristled with new equipment, encryption arrays that hadn't existed a week ago. Even the Bioweb felt different, its usual harmonious pulse overlaid with something sharper, more urgent. Data streams that had once carried agricultural reports and weather patterns now hummed with military frequencies.

Wakana Station, when she reached it, had been transformed. The organic curves of its architecture remained, but the atmosphere had hardened. Engineers moved with purpose rather than contemplation. Conversations stopped when she passed, resumed in hushed tones after she was gone. Everyone seemed to be waiting for something. Preparing for something.

In the central courtyard, a young engineer was struggling with a malfunctioning resonance calibrator, cursing softly as the device refused to sync. Aiyana almost stopped to help, then saw what the engineer was doing wrong: holding the calibrator too tightly, fighting it instead of letting it find its own balance.

The memory ambushed her: Kele, sixteen years old, making the same mistake with the same stubborn grip. Their father had watched for a full minute before finally saying, *"Son, that calibrator is not a snake. It will not bite you if you relax."*

Kele had laughed, embarrassed, and loosened his hold. The calibrator had synced immediately. After that, whenever either of them gripped something too tightly, whether a tool or an argument or a grudge, the other would whisper: *"Not a snake."*

The last time Aiyana had said it was during their argument before he left, when his certainty had seemed so rigid, so unyielding. He hadn't laughed. Had just looked at her with something sad in his eyes and said, *"Some things you have to grip tight, little bird. Or they slip away before you understand what they were."*

She walked past the struggling engineer without stopping, the joke turned to ash in her throat.

Elder Nayeli found her in the equipment bay, where she had

gone to return her traveling gear. The old woman looked older than Aiyana remembered, the lines around her eyes deeper, the set of her shoulders heavier.

"You're back," Nayeli said. It wasn't a question.

"The summit failed."

"We know. The reports came through yesterday. Chogan's assessment was... comprehensive." Nayeli paused. "He spoke highly of you. Said you conducted yourself with honor in difficult circumstances."

"Honor." Aiyana set down her pack with more force than necessary. "I watched them lie to our faces for five days. I watched them twist every truth we offered into evidence of our own failures. And I couldn't do anything about it."

"That is often what diplomacy feels like, from the inside." Nayeli moved to stand beside her, her gaze distant. "The council has been in session continuously since word of the summit's collapse arrived. There are factions calling for immediate retaliation. Others demanding we close the borders entirely. Some want to go public with everything we know about the tower attack, force international condemnation."

"And what does the council want?"

"The council wants what it always wants. Consensus. Balance. A path forward that doesn't require abandoning our principles." Nayeli's voice carried a note of weary frustration. "They'll find one, eventually. They always do. But until then, we prepare. We strengthen. We make ourselves ready for whatever comes next."

"What about the evidence?" Aiyana pulled the data chip from her pocket, the one Tomas had pressed into her hand as the tower fell. "The harmonic data from Tower Seven. The proof that we were attacked."

"Chogan presented it to the council this morning. Along with your analysis of the interference patterns." Nayeli met her eyes. "It's been classified. Restricted access. The council believes that releasing it publicly would force an escalation we're not ready for."

Aiyana stared at her. "They're suppressing it? After everything that happened?"

"They're not suppressing it. They're controlling when and how it becomes public." Nayeli's voice was patient, the tone of someone explaining a difficult truth. "If we release the evidence now, the Pale Cities will claim it was fabricated. Their propaganda machines will tear it apart, create doubt, muddy the waters until no one knows what to believe. We need to wait for the right moment. When releasing the truth will have maximum impact and minimum cost."

"And how many more people die while we wait for the right moment?"

The question hung between them, unanswerable. Nayeli looked away first.

"You've been reassigned," she said quietly. "Effective immediately. Border monitoring station, eastern sector. The council wants experienced engineers on the front lines, people who understand the technology and can detect any attempts at interference."

"The front lines." Aiyana absorbed this. "You're sending me to watch for the next attack."

"I'm sending you where your skills are needed most." Nayeli reached out and touched her shoulder, a gesture that was both formal and oddly tender. "You saw what happened at Tower Seven. You understand the threat better than almost anyone. If they try again, you might be the one who catches it in time."

It was an honor, Aiyana understood. A recognition of her abilities, her experience, her value to the defense of their society. But it didn't feel like an honor. It felt like exile. Like being sent to the edge of the world to watch for a darkness that was already spreading.

"When do I leave?"

"Tomorrow. Take today to rest. To see your mother." Nayeli paused. "She's been asking about you. And about Kele."

The name sent a pulse of pain through Aiyana's chest. Kele. Her brother, still somewhere in the Frontier, still unreachable, still lost in the gray lands between worlds. She had hoped the summit might bring news of him, some word through back channels, some confirmation that he was alive and well. Instead, she had nothing. Only silence and the growing certainty that the borders closing around her were also closing around him.

"Thank you, Elder," she said. "For everything."

"Don't thank me yet." Nayeli's smile was thin. "The hard part is just beginning."

* * *

Her mother's house felt smaller than Aiyana remembered.

It was the same structure it had always been, grown from living wood in the style of their people, its walls breathing gently with the rhythm of the Bioweb. But something had changed. Perhaps it was Aiyana who had changed, her sense of scale altered by five days in the hybrid architecture of Threshold, by glimpses of Pale City towers through transport windows, by the dawning awareness of how vast the world really was.

Takoda met her at the door, her silver-streaked hair loose around her shoulders, her eyes bright with a mixture of relief and anxiety. She embraced Aiyana tightly, holding on longer than usual, and Aiyana let her. Let herself be a daughter again, if only for a moment. Let the weight of everything she had seen and done slip away in the warmth of her mother's arms.

"I watched the broadcasts," Takoda said when she finally released her. "What they said about the summit. What they said about us."

"The broadcasts were lies."

"I know." Takoda led her into the main room, where a meal had been laid out, simple food that smelled like home. "I know our broadcasts told a different story. But somewhere between those two stories is what actually happened. And I need to hear it from you."

So Aiyana told her. Not everything, not the classified details or the secret communications with Elias, but the shape of it. The hope that had flickered on Day Four, when Chogan and Vane had seemed close to an agreement. The destruction of that hope on Day Five, when Drax's leak had poisoned everything. The silent departure at the end, when words had become meaningless and only the absence of violence had distinguished the summit's conclusion from a declaration of war.

Takoda listened without interrupting, her hands wrapped around a cup of tea that slowly cooled, untouched. When Aiyana finished, she was quiet for a long moment.

"Your father believed in diplomacy," she said finally. "He used to say that every conversation was a bridge, even the difficult ones. That as long as people were talking, they weren't fighting." She set down her cup. "He would have been proud of you. For trying. For believing it was worth trying."

"It wasn't worth trying." The bitterness surprised Aiyana, coming out sharper than she intended. "We accomplished nothing. Less than nothing. The people who wanted war are closer to getting it than they were before we started."

"You don't know that." Takoda's voice was gentle but firm. "You saw five days of a conflict that has been building for centuries. You met people on both sides who want something other than destruction. That knowledge matters. Those connections matter. Even if you can't see how, yet."

Aiyana thought of Elias, sitting alone in his quarters, searching through archives for truths his government wanted hidden. Thought of Councillor Vane, his face gray with grief as he watched his attempt at peace be dismantled. Thought of Captain Ford, whose eyes had held something other than hostility when he looked at Commander Speaks-Low.

Her mother was right. There were cracks in the Pale Cities' facade. People who doubted. People who questioned. People who might, given the right circumstances, choose something other than the path their leaders were setting.

But those cracks felt so small. And the forces pushing toward war felt so vast.

"Have you heard anything about Kele?" she asked, changing the subject to the question that had been burning in her since she arrived.

Takoda's expression shifted, the careful composure cracking slightly. "Nothing. I've sent messages through every channel I know. The bridge-builder networks, the Frontier communities, even some contacts your father maintained before he died." She shook her head. "It's like he's vanished. Like the Frontier swallowed him whole."

"He's alive." Aiyana said it with more certainty than she felt. "I would know if he wasn't. Through the Bioweb, through Sitala, through something. He's out there."

"I hope you're right." Takoda reached across the table and took her daughter's hand. "I hope he's alive and well and doing the work he believed in. But I also hope he knows that the borders are closing. That whatever freedom of movement he had before, it's disappearing. If he's going to come home, it needs to be soon."

Aiyana squeezed her mother's hand, feeling the fragility of the bones beneath the skin, the years of worry and loss that had worn her down. Takoda had already lost a husband to the conflict between their peoples. The thought of losing a son as well was more than anyone should have to bear.

"I'll find him," Aiyana said. "Somehow. I'll find a way to reach him and bring him home."

It was a promise she had no idea how to keep. But she made it anyway, because her mother needed to hear it, and because she needed to say it. Needed to believe that some things were still possible, even as the world contracted around them.

They ate together as the light faded outside, speaking of smaller things, ordinary things, the daily rhythms of life that continued even when larger events threatened to sweep everything away. For a few hours, Aiyana could pretend that nothing had changed. That the world was still the place she had grown up in, safe and certain and full of possibility.

But when she went to bed that night, in the room she had slept in as a child, she lay awake for hours, staring at the ceiling. The Bioweb hummed around her, its harmonics subtly different than they had been before the tower fell. The network was still healing, still adjusting to the loss of Tower Seven. It would take months, perhaps years, for the damage to fully repair.

And somewhere out there, the people who had caused that damage were preparing to cause more.

* * *

She left before dawn, slipping out of the house while her mother still slept.

It was easier that way. No prolonged goodbyes, no tears, no promises that might prove impossible to keep. She left a note on the kitchen table, simple words of love and reassurance, and stepped out into the gray light of early morning.

Sitala was waiting on the perch outside, her golden feathers dark in the pre-dawn dimness. The eagle stirred as Aiyana approached, spreading her wings in a gesture that was both greeting and readiness.

Flying? The question came through the bond, wordless but clear.

Flying, Aiyana confirmed. *East. To the border.*

The transport to the eastern sector was waiting at the station's edge, a small craft designed for utility rather than comfort. Aiyana boarded with her minimal luggage, found a seat by the window, and watched as the only home she had ever known fell away beneath her.

The flight took her over territory she had covered during her initiation, the same ridge where Tower Seven had once stood. The ruins were visible from the air, a scar on the landscape that had already begun to soften as the living wood decayed and the earth reclaimed what had been built upon it. In a year, there would be nothing left but a clearing. In a decade, even the clearing would be gone, swallowed by the forest's patient growth.

But the people who had died there would not return. The bonds that had been severed would not reform. Some losses were permanent, no matter how well the world healed around them.

The border station appeared as the sun crested the eastern peaks, a cluster of low buildings perched on a ridge overlooking the Frontier. It was not impressive. It was not meant to be. Its purpose was observation, vigilance, the quiet work of watching and waiting.

Aiyana disembarked into air that tasted different here, sharper, less fully integrated with the Bioweb's harmonics. The station was at the edge of the network's reach, the last point where full connection was possible before the gray silence of the ungoverned lands began.

The station commander met her at the landing platform, a weathered woman named Sera Windwalker who looked like she had spent most of her life in places exactly like this. Her handshake was firm, her gaze assessing.

"Engineer Waketah. We've been expecting you." She glanced at Sitala, circling overhead. "You're the one from Tower Seven."

"I was there when it fell."

"Good. Then you know what we're watching for." Sera turned and began walking toward the main building, clearly expecting Aiyana to follow. "The council thinks another attack is coming. They don't know when or where, but they're certain it will happen. Your job is to make sure we see it before it's too late."

"And if I do see it? If I detect interference?"

"You report it immediately. We have direct channels to the council now, bypassing normal communication protocols. If something happens out here, they'll know within minutes." Sera paused at the building's entrance, her expression grim. "Whether they'll be able to do anything about it is another question. But at least they'll know."

It wasn't reassuring. But Aiyana hadn't come here expecting reassurance. She had come because this was where her skills were needed. Where she might make a difference. Where watching and waiting was the only form of action available.

She followed Sera into the station, leaving the rising sun behind her. Ahead, through windows that faced east, the Frontier stretched away into haze and distance. Somewhere out there, her brother was living a life she couldn't imagine. Somewhere out there, people she had never met were making decisions that might determine whether she lived or died.

And somewhere, in the gray towers of Nova-Providence, a young man named Elias was searching for truths that his society wanted to keep buried.

She hoped he was careful. Hoped he understood the risks he was taking. Hoped the connection they had formed, fragile and unlikely as it was, might survive what was coming.

But hope, she was learning, was a luxury. The only thing she could control was her own attention, her own vigilance, her own determination to see clearly what others might miss.

She settled into her new quarters, unpacked her few belongings, and prepared to watch the border.

The Cold War had begun. And she was on its front line.

13

The Truth Beneath

Nova-Providence had never felt so suffocating.

Elias walked its familiar streets in the days after his return from Threshold, and everything seemed wrong. The buildings loomed higher than he remembered, their steel and glass facades reflecting a sky that was always the same shade of filtered gray. The Signal Mesh broadcasts played from every public screen, their cheerful narratives about progress and renewal now sounding hollow, scripted, like lines delivered by actors who no longer believed their parts.

He had been reassigned to archive duties at the Doctrine Hall, a position that should have been a demotion but felt instead like an opportunity. Keeper Drax had returned from the summit triumphant, her narrative of MNA aggression and Pale Cities resilience playing on every broadcast. Councillor Vane had retreated into political obscurity, his brief attempt at accommodation now cited as evidence of naivety at best, disloyalty at worst. The summit's failure had been transformed into a victory, proof that the Pale Cities had been right all along to distrust their neighbors.

And Elias, the junior cultural attaché who had witnessed it all, had been quietly reassigned to a basement office where he could do no harm.

They thought they were punishing him. They didn't realize they had given him exactly what he needed.

The Doctrine Hall archives were vast, centuries of accumulated records stored in climate-controlled vaults beneath the city's administrative district. Most of it was mundane: census data, agricultural reports, infrastructure maintenance logs. But scattered among the ordinary were the documents that mattered. The records that shaped how citizens understood their history, their identity, their place in the world.

Elias had been given access to the mundane sections, the files that no one cared about anymore. But access, he had learned, was often a matter of persistence rather than permission. Systems designed to keep people out were also systems designed by people, with all the oversights and assumptions that implied.

He began his search on his third day back, staying late after the other archivists had gone home, using his legitimate access as cover for explorations that were decidedly not legitimate. The first night, he found nothing. The second night, the same. But on the third night, he discovered the version control system.

Every document in the archive, he learned, maintained a hidden history. Not just the current version, but every previous version, every edit, every deletion. The system had been designed for accountability, a way to track changes and identify errors. It had never been intended as a tool for uncovering deliberate falsification.

But that was exactly what Elias intended to use it for.

* * *

The document that broke him was filed under "Historical

Incidents: Wind Spine Infrastructure."

He had been searching for the third citation from Keeper Drax's summit presentation, the one he had already identified as suspicious. The current version described a Wind Spine failure thirty years ago, a catastrophic malfunction that had resulted in significant damage to the surrounding area. It was presented as evidence of inherent instability in MNA technology, proof that their organic approach to infrastructure was fundamentally unreliable.

The version history told a different story.

Three edits had been made to the document in the past decade. The first, eight years ago, had changed the word "attack" to "incident." The second, five years ago, had removed an entire paragraph describing the involvement of Pale Cities military forces. The third, just days before the summit, had added the phrase "attributed to system instability" where the original had read "caused by external interference."

Elias pulled up the original version, his hands trembling slightly on the keyboard. The document that appeared on his screen was not a record of MNA failure. It was a record of Pale Cities aggression.

Thirty years ago, a Pale Cities military unit had crossed into MNA territory and attempted to seize control of a Wind Spine tower. The operation had been called "Reclamation," based on the doctrine that MNA technology was rightfully Pale Cities property, stolen by ancestors who had refused to share their discoveries. The attack had failed, repelled by MNA defenders, but not before significant damage had been done to the tower and its surrounding infrastructure.

The original document included casualty figures. Eight MNA citizens had died. Three Pale Cities soldiers had been killed, their bodies recovered and returned through diplomatic channels that had been carefully kept secret from the public.

Eleven deaths, erased from history. Transformed into evidence of MNA incompetence.

Elias sat back in his chair, staring at the screen, feeling something fundamental shift inside him. He had suspected. Had known, on some level, that Drax's presentation was built on lies. But seeing it, reading the original words that had been systematically erased and replaced, made it real in a way that suspicion never could.

His government had killed people. Had covered it up. Had then used the cover-up as evidence to justify further hostility. The lie was not an aberration. It was a foundation. A cornerstone of the narrative that every Pale Cities citizen had been taught to believe.

He copied the document, both versions, onto a personal storage device. Then he continued searching, driven now by something beyond curiosity. Something closer to compulsion.

If this lie existed, what else had been hidden?

* * *

He found the Settlement Charter at 3:00 in the morning, in a section of the archive that should have been far beyond his access level.

The security had been layered, encryption protocols wrapped around authentication requirements wrapped around physical access restrictions. But someone, somewhere, had made a mistake. Had left a backdoor open, perhaps for their own convenience. Had never imagined that a junior archivist with too much time and too many questions might find it.

The document that appeared on his screen was old. Centuries old, its digital preservation imperfect, some portions degraded beyond readability. But enough remained. More than enough.

It was the original agreement between the first colonists and the Indigenous nations who had permitted their settlement. The document that every Pale Cities citizen learned about in school, the foundation of their understanding of why the separation had occurred.

Except the version Elias had learned was not the version he was reading now.

The official history said that the colonists had been offered impossible terms. Restrictions on land use so severe that survival was barely possible. Requirements for cultural assimilation that would have erased their identity. A choice between submission and extinction, with no middle ground.

The original document said something different.

The colonists had been offered integration. Full membership in the emerging alliance of nations, with all the rights and responsibilities that entailed. They would have had to adapt, yes. Would have had to learn new ways of relating to the land and to each other. But they would not have been erased. They would have been welcomed.

And they had refused.

Not because the terms were impossible, but because they were unacceptable. Because accepting them would have meant acknowledging that the Indigenous nations had something to teach. That the colonists' way of doing things was not automatically superior. That compromise was not the same as surrender.

The document included the final exchange between the colonial representatives and the alliance negotiators. The words were formal, stilted with the conventions of their era, but their meaning was clear:

We cannot accept terms that place us beneath those we came to lead. We will find our own path, separate from yours, and prove through our achievements that we were right to refuse your offer.

Elias read the words three times, feeling each reading strip away another layer of the world he had been taught to believe in.

His ancestors had not been driven out. They had not been oppressed or persecuted or forced to flee. They had been offered a home and had refused it, because accepting would have required them to be equals rather than masters.

The entire history of the Pale Cities, the narrative of victimhood and resilience that defined their identity, was built on a choice. A choice to separate rather than integrate. A choice to build walls rather than bridges. A choice that had been made centuries ago and then hidden, transformed into something that looked like persecution rather than pride.

He copied the document. Then he sat in the darkness of the archive, surrounded by centuries of carefully curated lies, and tried to remember how to breathe.

* * *

Dawn found him walking the streets of Nova-Providence, the storage device heavy in his pocket.

The city was waking around him, citizens emerging from their residential blocks to begin another day of productive contribution to the renewal of their society. They moved with purpose, with confidence, with the certainty of people who knew their place in the world. They had been taught that they were the inheritors of a noble struggle, the descendants of people who had been wronged and had risen above their circumstances through hard work and determination.

None of them knew the truth. None of them suspected

that the story they had been told was a careful construction, designed to justify choices that had been made before any of them were born.

Elias watched them pass, feeling like a ghost among the living. He had crossed a threshold in the night, moved from suspicion to knowledge, from doubt to certainty. There was no going back. He could not unread what he had read. Could not unknow what he now knew.

The question was what to do with it.

He could do nothing. Could bury what he had found, delete the copies, return to his life as if the night had never happened. It would be safer. Easier. The path of least resistance, the choice that most people in his position would make.

But he thought of Aiyana, standing in the garden at Threshold, asking him if he knew what his people had done. Thought of Councillor Vane, his face gray with grief as he watched his attempt at peace be destroyed. Thought of his father, dying in the Frontier, his death classified and his questions never answered.

He could not do nothing. Could not be complicit in the lie simply by refusing to challenge it.

But he also could not act alone. The documents he had found were powerful, but power without a plan was just noise. He needed allies. Needed people who could help him understand what to do with what he had discovered, how to release it in a way that might actually make a difference.

He thought of the observatory network at Threshold, the old communication channels that had been built for conversations that official systems could not carry. Aiyana had shown him how to access it. Had offered him a way to reach her if he found something that mattered.

This mattered. This was the truth beneath all the other truths, the lie at the foundation of everything his society believed about itself.

He found a public terminal in a quiet corner of the city, one of the older units that still connected to legacy networks. The observatory channels were buried deep, accessible only to those who knew exactly where to look. He typed carefully, aware that what he was doing was treason by any definition his government would recognize.

Found the original Settlement Charter. Everything we were taught is wrong. Our ancestors chose separation. They were offered integration and refused. The entire history is a lie.

He hesitated before sending, his finger hovering over the key. Once he did this, there was no going back. He would be committed, irrevocably, to a path that led away from everything he had known.

He thought of his mother, her face when he had left for the summit, the compass she had pressed into his hand.

So you can always find your way home.

But home was not a place. It was a story. And the story he had been told was not true.

He pressed the key. The message vanished into the network, traveling through channels that no one monitored anymore, toward a woman who had every reason to hate him and had chosen instead to trust him.

Then he walked back into the city, into the life he could no longer believe in, and waited to see what would happen next.

* * *

His mother called that evening, her face appearing on his apartment's communication screen with the slightly distorted quality of a long-distance connection.

"You look tired," she said, her eyes searching his face with a mother's instinct for things unsaid. "The reassignment is difficult?"

"It's an adjustment." He kept his voice neutral, knowing that anything he said might be monitored, might be analyzed, might become evidence of something he could not yet name. "The archive work is interesting. Lots of old documents. History."

"Your father loved history." Her smile was sad. "He used to say that understanding where we came from was the key to understanding where we were going."

Elias felt something tighten in his chest. His father had loved history. Had spent years working in the Frontier, in the gray lands between civilizations. Had died there, in circumstances that remained classified, for reasons that had never been explained.

Had his father discovered something? Had he found the same truths that Elias was now uncovering? Was that why he had died?

"Mom," he said carefully, "do you still have Dad's things? His personal files, his notes?"

"Some of them. Most were taken by the Ministry after he died. Standard procedure, they said." Her expression flickered. "Why do you ask?"

"I've been thinking about him. About his work. About what he might have been trying to accomplish." Elias paused. "I'd like to see what you still have. When I can get away to visit."

His mother was quiet for a moment, her eyes holding something he couldn't quite read. Then she nodded slowly.

"Come when you can," she said. "There are things I've been meaning to show you. Things I wasn't sure you were ready for." She paused. "But I think maybe you are now."

The call ended, leaving Elias alone in his apartment with the weight of everything he had learned pressing down on him. His father had known something. Had been trying to do something. And someone had stopped him.

The compass sat on his desk, its needle pointing east as it always did. Toward home. Toward everything he had been taught to believe.

But east was also the direction of the MNA. The direction of Aiyana, standing on a border that was hardening with every passing day. The direction of truth, waiting to be found by those brave enough to seek it.

He picked up the compass and held it in his palm, feeling its familiar weight. His father had carried this once. Had used it to navigate the Frontier, the gray lands where neither civilization's rules fully applied.

Perhaps it was time to follow in his footsteps.

Perhaps it was time to find out what his father had died for.

14

The Sound of Silence

They called it a demonstration.

Captain Lucian Ford stood in the observation gallery of Research Installation Eight, watching technicians make final adjustments to equipment he didn't fully understand. The room was cold, climate-controlled to protect delicate machinery, but it wasn't the temperature that chilled him. It was the anticipation in the air, the barely suppressed excitement of people about to witness something they had been working toward for years.

"Captain Ford." A woman in a white coat approached. "I'm Director Chen. You've been selected as military liaison for this project. Your role will be to assess tactical applications."

"Tactical applications of what, exactly?"

Director Chen gestured toward the equipment below: crystalline structures in precise geometric patterns, connected by cables that pulsed with faint light, all focused on a central emitter that reminded him of a weapon's barrel.

"We call it the Nullwave. The MNA built their civilization on resonance, on systems that communicate through frequencies we've spent generations learning to understand." Her eyes gleamed. "The Nullwave speaks their language. And it tells their systems to stop."

"Stop doing what?"

"Everything." She checked her tablet. "Today's demonstration will target a section of their Bioweb network near the eastern border. The primary targets are the bonded animals. Their neural integration is more complete, more vulnerable. We expect significant casualties among them."

"You're going to kill their animals."

"We're going to demonstrate capability." Her tone sharpened. "The MNA needs to understand what we can do. What we will do, if they continue to threaten our interests."

Lucian wanted to object. But he had been in the military long enough to know when objections would change nothing. He chose to watch. Because someone needed to remember what happened here.

"Beginning countdown," a technician announced. "Nullwave activation in sixty seconds."

The equipment hummed to life. The crystalline structures began to glow with light that seemed somehow wrong, frequencies the human eye wasn't meant to perceive.

"Ten seconds."

He closed his eyes. He couldn't watch the moment itself.

"Activation."

The sound that followed was not loud. It was simply wrong, a frequency that shouldn't exist, a note the universe itself seemed to reject. Lucian felt it in his bones, in his teeth, in the deep places where instinct lived.

And then, silence. Not the absence of sound. The absence of harmony. A void where something living had been.

Director Chen was smiling as data scrolled across her tablet. "Perfect. Absolutely perfect."

Somewhere out there, animals were dying. People were screaming. And he had done nothing to stop it.

* * *

Aiyana was monitoring the eastern sensor array when the world ended.

Not the whole world. Just the Bioweb, the living network that had been the background music of her entire life. One moment, it was there. The next, it was screaming.

She felt it hit like a physical blow. Her hands flew to her temples, a cry escaping her lips. And through the bond, through the connection more intimate than any other, she felt Sitala die.

Not die. Not quite. But something close. The eagle's mind went white with pain, neural pathways burning as the frequencies sustaining their bond were torn apart.

AIYANA

The name was a scream in her mind, wordless and desperate, and then even that was gone, replaced by silence so absolute she thought she had gone deaf.

She was on the floor. She didn't remember falling. Around her, the monitoring station had erupted into chaos. Other engineers were collapsed at their stations. Alarms wailed, distant and muffled.

"Sitala!" She pushed herself up, limbs trembling. The bond was still there, but wounded, bleeding silence instead of connection.

She found her eagle behind the main building, crumpled against the base of a monitoring tower. Alive, chest rising and falling in rapid, shallow breaths, but her eyes were wrong.

Glazed. Unfocused.

Aiyana fell to her knees, gathering the bird into her arms, feeling the frantic flutter of a heartbeat too fast, too erratic. Through the bond, she sensed fragments of Sitala's consciousness trying to reassemble themselves.

Hurts, came the thought, weak and confused. *Everything hurts. What happened?*

I don't know, Aiyana thought back, pushing comfort through the connection. *But you're safe now. I'm here.*

Around her, the station was discovering the scope of what had happened. Twelve animals dead. Birds, mostly. A deer. A family of rabbits. Three people injured, their Bioweb connections strong enough to transmit the feedback into physical symptoms.

Station Commander Windwalker found her still holding Sitala. "We need to report this immediately. The council needs to know."

"They targeted the animals," Aiyana said, her voice hoarse. "Deliberately. This is what they built. The thing that destroyed Tower Seven. They've made it into a weapon."

"A weapon that targets our bonds. Everything that makes us who we are." The commander's voice was flat. "Get your eagle to medical. Then report to communications. The council will want to hear from someone who experienced this firsthand."

We survived, Sitala thought, the words fragile but present.

We survived, Aiyana agreed. *But others didn't. And we need to make sure this never happens again.*

* * *

The Council Chamber had not seen an emergency session in ten years.

Chogan Grayfeather sat in his designated position, watching

fury unite fifty-three representatives in a way he had rarely witnessed. Speaker Wren Tallgrass stood at the center, her voice carrying across the chamber.

"Twelve animals killed. Three people injured. This was murder, designed to cause maximum pain with minimum accountability." She paused. "The weapon they used targets the foundations of our society. If they can do this to a border station, they can do it to a city. To our capital. We cannot allow this capability to exist unchallenged."

"What are you proposing?" Elder Blackriver's voice was calm but tense. "A retaliatory strike? Open war?"

"I am proposing we acknowledge reality. Every day that weapon exists is a day we live under threat of extinction."

"And how do you eliminate that threat?" Blackriver shook her head. "We don't know where it is. They'll deny it exists. War is a gamble, and the stakes are everything we've built."

The chamber erupted in competing voices. Chogan listened, feeling the weight of thirty years pressing down. He had devoted his life to preventing exactly this moment.

He rose from his seat. The chamber gradually fell silent.

"Speaker Tallgrass is correct," he began. "This weapon represents an existential threat. Elder Blackriver is also correct. War fought blind, against an enemy who has prepared for decades, would be catastrophic." He paused. "I propose we find out what we're dealing with before we respond."

"You're proposing a reconnaissance mission," Tallgrass said. "Into Pale Cities territory."

"An intelligence operation. Small team. Covert insertion. Locate and document the weapon system, gather information about deployment capabilities, and return without engaging." He met her eyes. "No destruction. No sabotage. No provocation."

"And if the team is caught?"

"Then we face consequences. But there is no option without risk. The question is which risks we accept."

Blackriver rose. "I support the proposal. We cannot respond effectively to a threat we do not understand."

The vote was not unanimous. Fifteen opposed. But thirty-eight voted in favor.

The operation would be called Silent Measure.

* * *

After the session, Chogan remained in the empty chamber. Elder Blackriver found him there.

"You didn't tell them everything," she said.

"No."

"The young engineer. Waketah. You want her on the team."

"She survived Tower Seven. She experienced the Nullwave firsthand. She understands the technology." Chogan paused. "And she has contacts inside the Pale Cities. Someone sharing information with her. A young man who discovered his government has been lying about everything."

"You trust him?"

"I trust that he is genuinely disillusioned. He may be the only asset we have inside their society."

"You're sending Waketah into enemy territory to trust a source she's never met, to gather intelligence on a weapon that could kill her with a thought." Blackriver's voice was flat. "Does she know?"

"Not yet. I will give her the choice to refuse."

"She won't refuse."

"No." The certainty was tinged with regret. "She's young enough to still believe she can make a difference. Old enough to understand what's at stake. The perfect age for heroism, which is another word for accepting risks that older, wiser people would refuse."

Blackriver placed her hand on his arm. "We do what we must. For the people we serve. It doesn't make it easier. But it makes it necessary."

Chogan rose slowly. "I've been telling myself that for thirty years. It's never gotten easier."

He left to find Aiyana Waketah, to ask her to do the impossible.

Operation Silent Measure would launch in three days.

The outcome would determine whether the Cold War remained cold, or finally ignited into something that would consume them all.

15

Silent Measure

The briefing room was underground, carved into the living rock beneath Wakana Station.

Aiyana had not known it existed until Commander Speaks-Low led her through a series of doors that had appeared ordinary and turned out to be anything but. The security protocols were elaborate, the kind designed for operations that officially didn't happen, missions that would never appear in any public record.

She descended the final staircase with Sitala riding her shoulder, the eagle's presence a comfort after everything they had endured. The bond between them was still healing, still tender in places where the Nullwave had torn through their connection. But Sitala was strong, stronger than Aiyana had realized, and the eagle had made clear through wordless determination that she would not be left behind.

The room at the bottom was small and functional: a central table, chairs for perhaps a dozen people, walls that absorbed sound rather than reflecting it. Chogan Grayfeather was already there, his face drawn with exhaustion but his eyes sharp. Beside him stood a woman Aiyana didn't recognize, perhaps forty years old, with the weathered look of someone who had spent significant time in harsh conditions.

"Engineer Waketah." Chogan rose to greet her. "Thank you for coming."

"You said it was urgent."

"It is." He gestured toward the unfamiliar woman. "This is Renna Clearwater. She'll be part of the team I'm about to brief you on."

Renna nodded in acknowledgment, her expression guarded but not unfriendly. "I've heard about Tower Seven. About what you did there. Saving the data, getting out alive." She paused. "That took skill."

"It took luck."

"Luck helps. But you can't rely on it." Renna's smile was thin. "I spent fifteen years on the Frontier. The gray lands between our world and theirs. I know the routes, the hidden paths, the places where neither side's patrols look too carefully. If we're going where I think we're going, you'll need someone who knows how to move through territory that doesn't officially exist."

Aiyana looked at Chogan, understanding beginning to dawn. "You're sending us into the Pale Cities."

"Yes." He sat down heavily, gesturing for the others to do the same. "The council has authorized an intelligence operation. Codename: Silent Measure. The objective is to locate and document the weapon that was used against your border station. The Nullwave."

The word sent a chill through Aiyana, memories of screaming silence and Sitala's mind going white with pain. She felt the eagle tense on her shoulder, felt the echo of trauma that neither of them had fully processed.

"We don't know where it is," she said. "We don't even know what it looks like."

"That's what we need to find out." Chogan activated a display on the table's surface, projecting a map of Nova-Providence and its surrounding districts. "Our intelligence suggests the weapon is not a single installation. It's a network, distributed across multiple locations, integrated into the city's existing power infrastructure."

"How do you know that?"

"Because of information provided by a source inside the Pale Cities government." Chogan's eyes met hers steadily. "A source you've been in communication with."

Aiyana felt her face flush. "Elias. You know about Elias."

"I know that you established contact with a junior Pale Cities official at Threshold. That he has been sharing information with you through back channels. That his discoveries include significant revelations about his government's historical deceptions." Chogan paused. "I also know that he may be our best chance of finding what we're looking for."

"You want me to use him."

"I want you to contact him. To ask if he can help us understand where the Nullwave installations are located. If he's willing, he could provide intelligence that would save us weeks of searching. If he's not..." Chogan spread his hands. "Then we find another way."

Aiyana thought of Elias in the garden at Threshold, his face pale with the weight of what he was discovering. Thought of the messages he had sent since, each one revealing another layer of deception, another truth his government had tried to bury. He was risking everything to share what he had learned.

Asking him to do more felt like asking him to risk his life.

"He's not trained for this," she said. "He's a cultural attaché. A documentarian. If he tries to gather intelligence on something as classified as the Nullwave, they'll catch him."

"Possibly. That's why we're not asking him to gather intelligence. We're asking him to share what he already knows, and to help you navigate the city once you're inside." Chogan leaned forward. "The decision is yours, Aiyana. I won't order you to contact him, and I won't order you to go on this mission. The council has authorized Silent Measure, but participation is voluntary. You have the right to refuse."

"But you're asking me specifically."

"I'm asking you because you're qualified. Because you understand the technology better than almost anyone. Because you have a connection inside their society that no one else has." He paused. "And because I believe you want to do something more than watch from a border station while they build weapons that could destroy us all."

He was right. She hated that he was right. But sitting at that monitoring station, watching sensors and waiting for the next attack, had felt like slow suffocation. This was a chance to act. To do something that might actually matter.

"Who else is on the team?" she asked.

* * *

Commander Speaks-Low arrived an hour later, his presence filling the small room with quiet authority.

Aiyana had worked with him briefly during the summit, had seen him navigate the complex politics of diplomatic security with a calm that bordered on supernatural. Now, in this underground briefing room, that calm took on a different character. This was a man who had been in combat. Who had made decisions that determined whether people lived or died. Who was preparing to lead a team into enemy territory with no guarantee of return.

"The team is small by design," he said, taking his place at the head of the table. "Four people. Me, as team lead and security. Renna, as our guide through the Frontier and into Nova-Providence. Aiyana, as our technical expert and contact liaison." He paused. "Sitala will provide aerial reconnaissance where possible, though her range will be limited once we're inside the city."

"You said four people," Aiyana noted. "Who's the fourth?"

"A communications specialist. Kira Songwind. She's being briefed separately and will join us at the insertion point." Speaks-Low activated the map display, zooming in on the Frontier zone between MNA territory and the Pale Cities. "We'll cross here, through the ruins of the old industrial settlements. It's rough terrain, but Renna knows it well. From there, we make our way to the outskirts of Nova-Providence and establish contact with Aiyana's source."

"And then?"

"Then we find the Nullwave." He traced a path through the city's districts. "Our intelligence suggests the primary installation is somewhere in Sector Twelve, the industrial zone. But the network is distributed, which means there are components throughout the city. We need to locate enough of them to understand the system's architecture, its power requirements, its vulnerabilities."

"What about the people?" Renna asked. "The Pale Cities have citizens too. Families. Children. If this weapon is integrated into their power grid, destroying it would..."

"We're not there to destroy anything." Speaks-Low's voice

was firm. "The council was explicit: gather intelligence, do not engage. Our mission is to document and report, nothing more. Whatever decisions get made about the Nullwave, they'll be made by people with a full understanding of the consequences."

"And if we're discovered?" Aiyana asked. "If the Pale Cities catch us inside their borders, with evidence that we've been conducting espionage?"

"Then we've handed them a justification for whatever response they choose." Speaks-Low met her eyes steadily. "I won't pretend there's no risk. This mission could end badly in a dozen different ways. But the council believes that the risk of not knowing is greater than the risk of finding out."

Aiyana nodded slowly, accepting the weight of what he was saying. Then another question surfaced, one she had been avoiding since the briefing began.

"Commander," she said carefully, "are there MNA citizens in Pale Cities territory? People who might be affected by our presence there?"

Speaks-Low's expression flickered, something passing behind his eyes that might have been understanding. "You're asking about your brother."

"You know about Kele?"

"I know that Kele Waketah was a bridge-builder working in the Frontier. That he disappeared from contact approximately four months ago. That his last known position was along one of the crossing routes into Pale Cities territory." The commander's voice was careful, measured. "I also know that some bridge-builders have been... detained by Pale Cities authorities. Held for questioning about their activities and connections."

"Detained. You mean imprisoned."

145

"I mean that we don't know for certain what's happened to them. The Pale Cities don't acknowledge holding MNA citizens, and we have no way to verify independently." He paused. "If your brother is alive and in Pale Cities custody, this mission might bring us information about his whereabouts. But I need you to understand something, Aiyana. Finding Kele cannot be the mission's objective. If it comes down to a choice between completing our assignment and pursuing a personal rescue, the mission has to come first."

The words hit like a blow, even though she had known they were coming. She thought of Kele, somewhere in that gray city of steel and glass, not knowing if anyone was looking for him. Thought of her mother, waiting for news that never came. Thought of the promise she had made to bring him home.

"I understand," she said. The words felt like broken glass in her mouth.

"Good." Speaks-Low's voice softened slightly. "I'm not asking you to abandon hope. I'm asking you to be realistic about what this mission can accomplish. If there's a way to help your brother without compromising our objectives, we'll take it. But I need to know that you can keep your focus when the pressure hits."

"You can count on me, Commander."

He studied her for a long moment, then nodded. "I believe I can. That's why you're on this team."

* * *

The briefing continued for another three hours, covering routes, contingencies, communication protocols, and the dozen other details that separated a successful operation from a disaster.

By the time it ended, Aiyana's head was spinning with

maps and timelines and code phrases. She emerged from the underground room feeling like she had been submerged in deep water and was only now breaking the surface.

Chogan caught her in the corridor, his hand gentle on her arm.

"A moment, if you have it."

She stopped, waiting. The old diplomat looked tired beyond measure, the weight of decades visible in every line of his face.

"I want you to know," he said quietly, "that I don't send you on this mission lightly. I have spent my entire career trying to find paths that don't require people to risk their lives. But sometimes..." He trailed off, searching for words. "Sometimes the only path forward goes through danger. And when that happens, the best we can do is send the people most likely to survive it."

"You think we can survive this?"

"I think you're resourceful, intelligent, and motivated. I think Speaks-Low is one of the best field commanders we have. I think Renna knows the Frontier better than anyone alive." He paused. "And I think your contact inside the Pale Cities is genuine in his desire to help. That may matter more than any tactical advantage."

"Elias." Aiyana said the name softly. "You really think he'll help us?"

"I think he's already helped us, by sharing what he's discovered. I think he's on a path that leads away from his government and toward something he believes is right." Chogan's eyes held hers. "Whether that path leads all the way to active assistance, I don't know. That will be your job to determine. To reach out. To ask. To see if the connection you've built can bear the weight of what we need."

"And if it can't?"

"Then you find another way. Or you come home with whatever intelligence you've gathered, and we figure out the next step from there." He released her arm. "I'm not asking for miracles, Aiyana. I'm asking for your best effort. That's all any of us can give."

She nodded, not trusting herself to speak. Chogan turned and walked away, his footsteps fading into the station's ambient sounds. Aiyana stood alone in the corridor, Sitala a warm weight on her shoulder, her mind already racing through everything that needed to happen in the next seventy-two hours.

She had to contact Elias. Had to ask him for help that could cost him everything. Had to trust that the connection they had built through encrypted messages and shared revelations was strong enough to survive the weight of what she was about to request.

She found a secure terminal and composed her message with care, each word chosen for maximum clarity and minimum exposure.

Coming your way soon. Need your help finding something. It's the weapon. The one that makes silence. Can you help us locate it?

She hesitated before adding the final line, knowing what she was asking, knowing what it might cost him.

I wouldn't ask if there was another way.

She sent the message and waited, staring at the blank screen, hoping that somewhere in Nova-Providence a young man with a compass and a conscience would receive her words and choose to help.

In three days, Operation Silent Measure would begin.

In three days, she would cross into enemy territory and try

to find a weapon that could end everything she loved.

In three days, she would see Elias face to face for the first time since Threshold, and learn whether trust built through words could survive the weight of action.

She hoped it could.

She hoped a lot of things.

Hope, she was learning, was all any of them had left.

16

The Point of No Return

The message arrived at midnight, when Elias was alone in his apartment, surrounded by copies of documents that could get him executed.

He had been careful. Had learned to access the observatory network only from public terminals, only at odd hours, only after ensuring no one was watching. But the message that appeared on his personal device, bypassing every security protocol he had established, made clear that careful was no longer enough.

Coming your way soon. Need your help finding something. It's the weapon. The one that makes silence. Can you help us locate it?

He read the words three times, his heart pounding against his ribs. Aiyana was coming to Nova-Providence. Was asking him to help find the Nullwave. Was asking him to cross a line that he could never uncross.

I wouldn't ask if there was another way.

He sat in the darkness of his apartment, the glow of the message the only light, and tried to think clearly. Everything he had done so far, the archive searches, the document copying, the messages to Aiyana, could be explained as intellectual curiosity. Misguided, perhaps. Inappropriate, certainly. But not treasonous. Not the kind of thing that warranted execution.

This was different. This was actively helping an enemy intelligence operation. This was providing information that could be used against his own people. This was choosing sides in a way that could never be taken back.

He thought of his mother, who had already lost a husband to the conflict between their peoples. Thought of what it would do to her if she lost a son as well, not to an accident in the Frontier but to a firing squad in Nova-Providence.

He thought of the twelve animals that had died in the Null-wave test. The creatures who had done nothing wrong except exist in connection with people who loved them. He thought of the weapon that had killed them, hidden somewhere in this city, waiting to be used again on a larger scale.

He thought of the Settlement Charter, the original agreement that proved his ancestors had chosen isolation over equality. Had built an entire civilization on the refusal to accept that others might be their equals.

And he thought of Aiyana, standing in the garden at Threshold, asking him if he knew what his people had done. The question that had started everything. The question he was finally ready to answer.

Yes, he knew. And knowing meant he could not do nothing.

He composed his reply with trembling fingers, aware that each word was another step toward a point of no return.

I'll help. Don't know where the weapon is, but I know people who might. Will gather what I can. When do you arrive?

He sent it before he could change his mind. Then he sat in the darkness, waiting for a response that might not come, committed to a path that led away from everything he had known.

* * *

The knock on his door came three days later, just after sunset.

Elias had spent those days in a state of controlled panic, continuing his archive work by day, searching for any information about the Nullwave by night. He had found fragments: budget allocations to unnamed research projects, personnel transfers to facilities that didn't appear on any official map, encrypted communications that he couldn't access but whose very existence suggested something being hidden.

But he had found nothing concrete. Nothing that would tell Aiyana where to look, what to document, how to complete whatever mission she had been sent to accomplish.

The knock was soft but insistent, the kind that expected an answer. Elias approached his door with his heart in his throat, half-expecting to find Doctrine Office security on the other side, come to arrest him for the crimes he had already committed and the ones he was planning to commit.

Instead, he found Captain Lucian Ford.

The security officer stood in the corridor, alone, dressed in civilian clothes rather than his usual uniform. His face was unreadable, but something in his eyes suggested he wasn't here in any official capacity.

"Harren," he said. "May I come in?"

Elias hesitated, his mind racing through possibilities. Ford had been at Threshold. Had been part of the security team, answering to Keeper Drax. If he was here to arrest Elias, he would have brought reinforcements. If he was here to threaten him, to warn him off whatever path he was on, civilian clothes would make more sense.

But there was something else in Ford's expression. Something that looked almost like the same uncertainty Elias had been feeling since Threshold. The same questioning. The same doubt.

"Come in," he said, stepping aside.

Ford entered the apartment, his eyes sweeping the space with professional assessment before settling on the documents spread across Elias's desk. He didn't comment on them. Didn't ask what Elias was researching or why. He simply took a seat in the apartment's only chair and waited for Elias to close the door.

"I'm not here officially," Ford said. "No one knows I'm here. No one will know we spoke. If you tell anyone about this conversation, I'll deny it happened."

"Understood." Elias remained standing, keeping distance between them. "What do you want?"

"To ask you a question." Ford's eyes met his steadily. "At Threshold, after the summit collapsed, you spoke with Councillor Vane in the garden. I saw you from the terrace. You talked for some time, and when you left, Vane looked like a man who had just been told something he needed to hear."

Elias felt cold sweat break out along his spine. "I don't know what you mean."

"Don't." Ford's voice was quiet but firm. "Don't insult me by pretending. I've spent fifteen years learning to read people. I know when someone is lying, and I know when someone is carrying a weight they can't bear alone." He paused. "You've found something. Something that shook you badly enough to approach a senior councillor and share it with him. I want to know what it was."

"Why?"

153

"Because I've found things too." Ford leaned forward, his voice dropping. "Three days ago, I was brought to a research installation that doesn't officially exist. I watched them test a weapon that turns silence into death. I watched them kill animals just to prove they could, and then I watched them celebrate like they'd won a war instead of committed murder."

Elias stared at him, pieces clicking into place. "You were there. When they tested the Nullwave."

"I was there." Ford's jaw tightened. "And I couldn't do anything about it. Couldn't stop it, couldn't warn anyone, couldn't do anything except watch and remember. They brought me there to assess tactical applications. To figure out how to use that weapon in the field." His voice cracked slightly. "I have a daughter, Harren. Eight years old. She loves animals. Loves them more than anything. And I stood in that room and watched them die, and I thought about what kind of world I'm helping to build for her."

The silence stretched between them, filled with the weight of shared horror and shared doubt.

"The documents I found," Elias said slowly, "prove that our government has been lying to us for centuries. About the separation. About the MNA. About everything that justifies our existence as a separate society." He paused. "I don't know what to do with that knowledge. I don't know how to make it matter."

"Neither do I." Ford sat back. "But I know that doing nothing isn't an option anymore. Not after what I've seen. Not after what they're planning."

"What are they planning?"

"The test was successful. The weapon works. The next step is deployment." Ford's eyes were haunted. "They're going to use it, Harren. Not as a demonstration. As an attack. On MNA cities. On their food production. On anything and everything that depends on the connections they've built." He paused. "Unless someone stops them."

"How? How does anyone stop something like that?"

"I don't know yet. But I'm working on it." Ford rose from the chair, moving toward the door. "I'm telling you this because I need to know I'm not alone. Because I saw your face at the summit, and I recognized something in it. The same thing I've been feeling ever since I watched that weapon fire."

"What's that?"

"The knowledge that we're on the wrong side." Ford paused at the door. "And the understanding that knowing isn't enough. That eventually, we're going to have to choose whether to do something about it."

He left without another word, disappearing into the corridor, leaving Elias alone with the weight of everything that had just been said.

* * *

Aiyana's response arrived an hour later.

Three days. Coming through the Frontier. Will contact you when we're inside. Need safe place to meet. Can you arrange?

Elias read the message, feeling the weight of it settle into his chest. Three days. In three days, an MNA team would be inside Nova-Providence, and he would be their only contact. Their only source of local knowledge. Their only hope of finding what they were looking for.

He thought of Captain Ford, his face haunted by what he had witnessed. Thought of the weapon that was waiting somewhere in this city, ready to be used again. Thought of the documents on his desk, the proof that everything his people believed was built on lies.

And he thought of his father, who had died in the Frontier, whose death had never been explained, whose questions had never been answered.

His mother had said there were things she wanted to show him. Things she hadn't thought he was ready for. Perhaps now was the time.

He composed his reply carefully, aware that each word was another step into territory from which there was no return.

I can arrange it. There's a district in the old industrial zone. Sector Four. Fewer patrols, more abandoned buildings. I'll have a location by the time you arrive.

He paused, then added:

I've made contact with someone inside the security apparatus. Someone who saw the weapon tested and wants to help. He may have information about where it's located. I'll know more soon.

He sent the message and sat back, staring at the blank screen. He had just committed to helping an enemy operation. Had just agreed to guide MNA agents through his own city. Had just revealed that he was building a network of dissent within the Pale Cities government.

If anyone intercepted these messages, if anyone traced them back to him, he would be dead within days. Executed as a traitor. His name erased from the records, his memory consigned to the same historical amnesia that had swallowed so many uncomfortable truths.

But he couldn't stop now. Couldn't unsend what he had sent. Couldn't unknow what he knew.

He pulled his father's compass from his pocket and held it in his palm. The needle trembled, then steadied, pointing east as it always did. Toward home. Toward Nova-Providence. Toward the life he was about to betray.

But east was also the direction from which Aiyana would come. The direction of the MNA. The direction of the people his government was planning to destroy with a weapon that turned silence into death.

His father had carried this compass into the Frontier. Had used it to navigate the gray lands between civilizations. Had died there, for reasons that remained classified, in circumstances that had never been explained.

Perhaps his father had discovered the same truths. Perhaps he had tried to do something about them. Perhaps that was why he had died.

Elias closed his fist around the compass and made a silent promise to the man who had given it to him.

I'm going to finish what you started, he thought. *Whatever it takes. Whatever it costs. I'm going to find the truth and make it matter.*

Three days.

In three days, everything would change.

He just hoped he would live long enough to see what came after.

17

Into the Gray

The Frontier began where the Bioweb ended.

Aiyana felt the transition like a physical sensation: the harmonic hum that had accompanied her entire life simply stopped. On her shoulder, Sitala shifted uneasily, confusion and fear threading through their bond.

Strange, Sitala thought. *Empty. Don't like it.*

I know, Aiyana replied. *But we have to go through it.*

They traveled for two days through the gray lands, moving by night and sheltering by day in ruins that spoke of a different philosophy of construction. These structures hadn't been grown. They had been built from separate pieces, and now they were falling apart, unable to maintain themselves.

Renna led them along paths that avoided both MNA and Pale Cities patrols. Occasionally they passed other travelers, gray figures who acknowledged them with silent nods. The Frontier had its own code: don't ask questions, don't offer information, don't make yourself memorable.

On the second night, they reached the edge of Pale Cities territory. The ruins gave way to maintained roads, the wilderness to ordered fields, the silence to the distant hum of industrial activity.

"There." Renna pointed toward lights on the horizon. "Nova-Providence. Thirty kilometers."

Somewhere in that city, Elias was waiting. Somewhere in that city, the Nullwave was hidden. Somewhere in that city, her brother might be imprisoned.

"Let's go," Aiyana said. "We've waited long enough."

Speaks-Low caught her arm. "We move when the patrol cycles shift. Not before."

She wanted to argue. Every hour of waiting felt like failure, like twelve dead animals and a brother who might be dying while she crouched in ruins doing nothing. But she had learned something in the weeks since Tower Seven fell. Recklessness killed. Patience saved lives.

She sat down to wait, and hated every minute of it.

* * *

The maintenance tunnels were cramped, dark, and unpleasant, but they got the team inside Nova-Providence's industrial district by midnight.

Sitala had remained outside, unable to navigate the confined space. She would find her way to Aiyana through the urban landscape, guided by their bond. The separation felt wrong, but there was no alternative.

When they emerged into the city proper, Aiyana looked up at towers of steel and glass, their surfaces reflecting artificial light that turned night into perpetual twilight. The city never slept. It ran on constant motion, constant production, constant consumption.

"The rendezvous point is two kilometers east," Speaks-Low said. "We have three hours. Let's use them to scout the area."

They moved through enemy streets like ghosts, four MNA operatives in a city that would kill them if it knew they were there.

* * *

The abandoned processing facility smelled of rust and forgotten purpose.

Aiyana moved through its empty halls with Sitala riding her shoulder, the eagle having found her way through the urban maze. The team had arrived an hour early, deployed in a loose perimeter, ready to disappear if the rendezvous turned out to be a trap.

She didn't believe it was a trap. But belief and certainty were different things.

"Movement," Kira's voice came through her earpiece. "Single figure. Matches the description."

Elias Harren emerged from the shadows, moving with careful deliberation. He was taller than she remembered from Threshold, or perhaps that was just the effect of seeing him in his own environment. He stopped ten meters away, his eyes finding hers in the dim light.

"You came," he said. His voice carried the strain of sleepless nights.

"I said I would."

"I've spent so long sending messages into the void. Having you actually here feels like something from a dream." He paused. "Or a nightmare. I'm not sure which."

"Probably both." She allowed herself a small smile. "Dreams and nightmares often look the same until you wake up."

His gaze shifted to Sitala. "Your eagle. I've never seen one up close. They don't exist in the Pale Cities anymore."

"Her name is Sitala. She's why I survived the Nullwave test."

The mention of the Nullwave brought them back to why they were here. Elias's expression hardened.

"I've found things. Not everything, but enough to point you in the right direction."

* * *

They gathered in what had once been the facility's control room. Elias activated a small device, projecting a map of Nova-Providence.

"The Nullwave isn't a single installation. It's a network, distributed across the city's power infrastructure." He pointed to a location in Sector Twelve. "The main control center is here. Research Installation Eight. Officially, it doesn't exist."

"How do we get in?" Speaks-Low asked.

"Not through the front door. Multiple checkpoints, biometric access, armed guards." Elias zoomed the map to show underground lines. "But the Nullwave draws enormous power. They built dedicated conduits from auxiliary power stations. Large enough for maintenance access, minimal security."

"They keep underestimating what people will do when they're desperate enough," Renna observed.

"The conduits get you close. But the last hundred meters into the installation itself, that's where it gets dangerous. Internal security. Motion sensors. Automated defenses." Elias hesitated. "And there's someone who can help. Captain Lucian Ford. Border Guard. He was at the installation when they tested the Nullwave. He saw what it did, and it broke something in him."

"Can we trust him?"

"He has a daughter. He's terrified of the world they're building for her." Elias spread his hands. "I've been wrong about people before. But I think he's genuine."

Speaks-Low turned to Aiyana. "Your assessment?"

She considered carefully. Everything tracked with what they had observed. "I believe him. Whether that's enough to base a mission on, I can't say. But we didn't come all this way to turn back at the first uncertainty."

"No," Speaks-Low agreed. "We didn't. Can you arrange a meeting with Ford tonight?"

Elias nodded. "I'll contact him."

* * *

While Elias sent his message, Aiyana found a moment alone with him near a broken window. The city lights spread before them, a sea of artificial brightness.

"Can I ask you something?" she said. "Not about the mission."

He turned, surprised. "What?"

"What was it like? Growing up here, I mean. Before you knew." She gestured at the towers. "Was it a good life?"

Elias was quiet for a moment. "It was comfortable. Ordered. I knew exactly what was expected of me, exactly what path my life would take. There's a kind of peace in that." He paused. "But there were always cracks. Questions that didn't have good answers. My father asking too many of them before he died. The way certain topics made people go quiet."

"What would you build? If you could change it?"

He considered. "Something honest. A society that didn't need lies to hold itself together. Where people could ask questions without disappearing." A bitter smile. "I don't know if that's possible. But I'd like to find out."

"That sounds like something my brother would say."

"The bridge-builder?"

"Kele." She kept her voice steady. "He disappeared four

162

months ago, working in the Frontier. Our intelligence suggests some bridge-builders have been detained. Held somewhere in Nova-Providence." She met his eyes. "I know it's not part of the mission. But if there's any chance he's alive..."

Elias pulled out his father's compass, the one artifact he had kept. "My father died in the Frontier. They said equipment failure. But I've found documents suggesting he was killed because he discovered something they wanted hidden." He looked at her. "I know what it's like to carry questions no one will answer."

"You'll help me look?"

"The information would be in the Doctrine Office archives. The same ones I've been searching for months." His jaw tightened. "I'll find what I can. I can't promise it will be what you want to hear."

"Thank you. For everything. The risks you've taken, the things you've shared. You didn't have to do any of it."

"Yes, I did." His voice was soft but certain. "When you discover everything you believed is a lie, you only have two choices. Accept the lie and keep living in it, or reject it and try to build something true." He put the compass away. "I couldn't accept it."

"No," she agreed. "Neither could I."

His communicator chirped. "Ford. He'll meet us in two hours. He has information about the installation's internal security."

Aiyana felt hope stir, fragile but present. The mission was still impossibly dangerous. But they had allies now. People inside the system who had seen the truth and chosen to act.

"Then let's go meet him," she said. "The sooner we know what we're dealing with, the sooner we can end it."

They gathered the team and slipped back into the streets of

Nova-Providence, moving toward a meeting that might give them what they needed.

The hunt for the Nullwave had begun.

18

The Soldier's Choice

Captain Lucian Ford had spent fifteen years learning to read rooms.

The basement of the workers' dormitory was small, cramped, and smelled of industrial cleaning agents. Not an ideal location for a clandestine meeting with enemy operatives, but ideal wasn't available. What mattered was that the building's surveillance had been offline for two weeks, pending maintenance that the bureaucracy had yet to authorize. In a society that ran on efficiency, the gaps in that efficiency were where people like him had learned to operate.

He arrived first, as he always did. Positioned himself with his back to the wall and clear sightlines to both exits. Old habits, drilled into him during his first years in the Border Guard. The habits that had kept him alive through situations that should have killed him.

The MNA team arrived in pairs, moving with the careful coordination of people who had trained together. The commander came first, a man whose stillness spoke of combat experience and whose eyes missed nothing. Then two women, one with the weathered look of someone who had spent years in harsh conditions, the other carrying communications equipment in a way that suggested she knew how to use it as more than just a radio.

And finally, the young engineer. The one Elias had told him about. The one who had survived the Nullwave test and carried an eagle on her shoulder like something out of legends his grandmother used to tell.

The eagle's eyes found his immediately, golden and fierce and impossibly aware. Lucian had never seen a bonded animal up close. Had been taught that such bonds were primitive, a remnant of less civilized times. But there was nothing primitive about the intelligence in that gaze. Nothing uncivilized about the way the bird and its human moved as one, each aware of the other without visible communication.

"Captain Ford." The commander's voice was neutral, professional. "I'm told you have information that might help us."

"That depends on what you're trying to accomplish." Lucian kept his own voice equally neutral. "Harren said you're looking for the Nullwave. That you want to document it, understand it. That you're not here to destroy anything."

"That's correct."

"Then yes. I have information that might help." Lucian paused, weighing his next words. "But first I need to understand something. If you find what you're looking for, if you document everything and get out safely, what happens next? What does your government do with the intelligence?"

The commander exchanged a glance with the young engineer before answering. "That decision isn't ours to make. We report what we find. The council decides what to do with it."

"And if they decide to go public? To share the evidence

internationally? To demand that the Nullwave be dismantled?"

"Those are possible outcomes."

"And if the Pale Cities refuse? If they deny everything and escalate instead?"

"Also possible." The commander's eyes were steady. "I won't lie to you, Captain. What we're doing here could lead to war. Could make everything worse instead of better. But doing nothing will definitely make things worse. The weapon you saw tested is just the beginning. They're planning to use it on a much larger scale. Cities. Food production. The foundations of our entire society."

Lucian nodded slowly. He had suspected as much. Had seen the gleam in Director Chen's eyes when she talked about tactical applications, about bringing the MNA to its knees. The test had been proof of concept. The deployment would be genocide dressed up as military strategy.

"Alright," he said. "Let me tell you what I know."

* * *

He talked for nearly an hour, laying out everything he had learned during his time as military liaison to the Quiet Choir's project.

The installation's layout, as far as he had been able to map it. The rotation schedules of the guard shifts. The locations of the automated defense systems, the ones that would trigger if anyone entered without proper authorization. The control room where the Nullwave's targeting and power systems were managed, buried three levels below the surface.

"The power conduits are your best approach," he confirmed, echoing what Elias had told them. "But they'll only get you to the outer perimeter of the installation. The last hundred meters are covered by motion sensors, pressure plates, and armed response teams on constant standby."

"How do we get through?" the engineer asked. She had been listening intently, her eagle occasionally shifting on her shoulder as if responding to her thoughts.

"There's a maintenance window. Every twenty-four hours, they run a full diagnostic on the sensor grid. Takes about fifteen minutes, during which the automated systems go into standby mode to avoid false positives from the testing equipment." Lucian pulled out a small device and activated a timer display. "The next window is in approximately eighteen hours. If you can reach the outer perimeter by then, you'll have to move quickly through the dead zone and reach the installation's service entrance."

"And then?"

"Then you'll need this." He reached into his jacket and pulled out a small card, the kind that served as identification and access authorization throughout Pale Cities facilities. "My credentials. They'll get you through the service entrance and into the lower levels. Won't work on the control room itself, that requires biometric confirmation, but they'll get you close enough to see what you need to see."

The commander took the card, examining it with careful fingers. "This is your access. If we use it, they'll know you helped us."

"I know."

"You'll be executed. Your family will be investigated. Every-thing you've built will be destroyed."

"I know." Lucian's voice was steady, though something flickered in his eyes. "My daughter is eight years old. She loves animals. Loves them more than anything in the world." He paused. "There are no animals left in Nova-Providence.

No birds, no deer, no foxes. They were all driven out or killed off generations ago, because they didn't serve any productive purpose. Because efficiency demanded that every resource be allocated to useful ends."

He looked at the eagle on the engineer's shoulder, and something like longing crossed his face.

"I've been teaching her that this is normal. That a world without animals is just how things are. That the pictures in her storybooks are fantasies, things that never really existed." His jaw tightened. "And then I stood in a room and watched them test a weapon designed to kill the last animals on this continent. Watched them cheer when the telemetry confirmed successful termination."

"Captain..." the engineer began, but he held up a hand.

"I can't undo what I've done. Can't bring back the creatures that died in that test. But I can choose what I do next." He met the commander's eyes. "I'm choosing to help you. Not because I think you're right about everything. Not because I've suddenly decided the MNA is perfect and the Pale Cities are evil. But because what they're building in that installation is wrong. Wrong in a way that goes beyond politics, beyond ideology, beyond anything I was taught to believe."

"And your daughter?"

"I've made arrangements." Lucian's voice was rough. "If things go wrong, she'll be taken somewhere safe. People I trust, outside the normal channels. She won't grow up knowing her father was a traitor." He paused. "Or maybe she will, someday. And maybe she'll understand why."

The room was silent for a long moment. Then the engineer stepped forward, her eagle shifting to maintain balance, and extended her hand.

169

"I'm Aiyana," she said. "Aiyana Waketah. And this is Sitala." The eagle dipped her head in what might have been acknowledgment. "Thank you, Captain. For everything you're risking. For everything you're giving up."

Lucian took her hand, feeling the strength in her grip, the calluses that spoke of work with her hands. "Don't thank me yet," he said. "Thank me if you make it out alive. Thank me if what you find makes a difference."

"We'll make it matter," she said. "Whatever we find. However this ends. We'll make it matter."

He believed her. Against all reason, against everything his training had taught him about trusting enemies, he believed her.

Maybe that was what choosing a side really meant. Not believing that one side was perfect, but believing that some things were worth fighting for regardless of which flag flew over them.

* * *

They finalized the plan in the hours before dawn.

Elias would guide them to the power conduit access point, using his knowledge of the city's infrastructure to avoid patrol routes. Renna would lead the team through the conduits themselves, navigating the kilometers of electrical infrastructure that separated the city from the installation. Kira would establish a relay point midway through, allowing them to maintain communication with their extraction route.

And Aiyana would enter the installation itself, using Ford's credentials to access the lower levels, documenting everything she could find about the Nullwave's architecture and capabilities.

"You're the only one with the technical expertise to understand what you're seeing," Speaks-Low explained when she questioned why she was being sent alone into the most dangerous part of the mission. "The rest of us would be looking at equipment without knowing what matters and what doesn't. You'll know."

"And if I'm caught?"

"Then you're caught. And we extract without you, because the intelligence you've already gathered is more important than any single person." His voice was gentle but implacable. "That's the reality of this operation, Aiyana. We're all expendable. What matters is the mission."

She nodded, accepting the weight of what he was saying. She had known the risks when she agreed to this. Had known that she might not come back. But hearing it stated so baldly made it real in a way that abstractions never could.

"Sitala will stay with the relay point," she said. It hurt to say it, hurt to contemplate separation, but the eagle couldn't navigate the tight confines of the conduits, and bringing her into the installation would only increase the risk of detection. "She can provide aerial reconnaissance for the extraction if things go wrong."

Through the bond, she felt Sitala's protest. *Don't like it. Want to stay with you.*

I know, Aiyana thought back. *But this is how it has to be. I'll come back to you. I promise.*

You better, Sitala replied, her thoughts carrying a fierce intensity. *Or I'll find you myself and drag you out.*

Despite everything, Aiyana smiled.

Ford left first, slipping back into the city he had served for fifteen years, the city he was about to betray in the most fundamental way possible. Elias went with him partway, the two men walking side by side in silence, united by choices they could never take back.

The team found places to rest in the dormitory basement, taking shifts to watch for any sign that they had been discovered. The hours until the operation began stretched ahead of them, each minute heavy with anticipation and dread.

Aiyana lay in the darkness, Sitala perched nearby, and tried to sleep. The city hummed around them, vast and indifferent, unaware that its deepest secrets were about to be exposed.

In eighteen hours, she would be inside Research Installation Eight.

In eighteen hours, she would see the Nullwave with her own eyes.

In eighteen hours, she would either find what they needed to stop a war, or she would die trying.

She closed her eyes and thought of Kele, somewhere in this city of steel and silence. Thought of her mother, waiting for news that might never come. Thought of Tower Seven and the fourteen who had died, whose deaths had set all of this in motion.

She thought of Elias and his compass, always pointing toward a home that no longer existed. Of Ford and his daughter, who loved animals in a world that had forgotten what animals were for. Of everyone on both sides who wanted something other than the war that seemed increasingly inevitable.

And finally, mercifully, she slept.

Tomorrow would come soon enough. And with it, everything would change.

19

The Heart of Silence

The power conduits hummed with energy that Aiyana could feel in her teeth.

She moved through the narrow tunnel in a half-crouch, her hands occasionally brushing the walls that thrummed with the pulse of Nova-Providence's electrical grid. The air was warm, almost uncomfortably so, and carried the sharp smell of ozone and heated metal. Every few meters, cables thicker than her arm ran along the ceiling, carrying enough power to light entire districts.

Ahead of her, Renna's silhouette navigated the darkness with the surety of someone who had done this before. Behind her, Speaks-Low moved in silence, his presence detectable only by the occasional scuff of boot on metal. Kira had stayed at the relay point two kilometers back, maintaining their communication link to the extraction route.

And Sitala was waiting at the surface, her thoughts a constant presence at the edge of Aiyana's awareness. The bond stretched thin over distance, but it held. It always held.

"Five hundred meters," Renna whispered, her voice barely

audible over the electrical hum. "The conduit opens into a junction chamber. From there, we can access the maintenance corridor that runs to the installation's outer perimeter."

"Time?" Speaks-Low's voice was equally quiet.

"Twenty-three minutes until the diagnostic window opens."

They pressed on, the tunnel narrowing slightly as they approached the junction. Aiyana felt her heart rate climbing, the familiar surge of adrenaline that came before any high-stakes operation. She had experienced it at Tower Seven, in the moments before everything went wrong. She hoped this time would end differently.

The junction chamber was larger than the conduit, a circular space where multiple power lines converged before continuing toward their destinations. Renna led them to a service hatch on the far wall, its surface marked with warning symbols in the angular script of Pale Cities industrial signage.

"This is where I leave you," Speaks-Low said quietly. "The corridor beyond is too exposed for a three-person team. Aiyana goes alone from here."

Aiyana nodded, having known this moment was coming. She checked her recording equipment one final time, ensuring the small device was secure against her chest, its lens positioned to capture whatever she encountered.

"If I'm not back in twenty minutes, assume I'm compromised," she said. "Don't wait. Get the team out."

"Understood." Speaks-Low's hand briefly gripped her shoulder. "But come back. That's an order."

"Yes, Commander."

She turned to the hatch, drew a breath, and stepped through.

* * *

The maintenance corridor was exactly as Ford had described:

narrow, utilitarian, and designed for workers who weren't expected to linger.

Aiyana moved quickly, counting her steps, tracking time in her head. Fifteen minutes until the diagnostic window opened. Fifteen minutes of motion sensors and automated defenses, watching for any intrusion that might trigger alarms she couldn't silence.

The corridor terminated at a heavy door marked with more warning symbols and a card reader that glowed faintly green in the dim light. Ford's credentials. The moment of truth.

She pressed the card to the reader and held her breath.

A soft chime. The light shifted from green to blue. The door clicked open.

Beyond was a small antechamber, empty except for a security station that stood unmanned. Ford had said the diagnostic window would draw most personnel to the control room, leaving the outer areas understaffed. He had been right. So far.

Aiyana crossed the antechamber and found the stairwell that led down into the installation's lower levels. Three floors below, according to Ford's briefing, lay the heart of the Nullwave: the control room where the weapon's targeting systems were managed, and the generator array that powered the entire network.

She descended, each step taking her deeper into enemy territory, further from safety, closer to the thing that had killed twelve animals and wounded Sitala's mind.

The first sublevel was administrative. Offices, empty now, their occupants presumably monitoring the diagnostic from the control room. The second sublevel housed the power distribution systems, massive transformers that hummed with barely contained energy. The third sublevel...

The third sublevel was the Nullwave.

Aiyana emerged from the stairwell and stopped, her breath catching in her throat.

The chamber before her was vast, far larger than any space she had imagined existing beneath Nova-Providence's streets. It stretched away in all directions, its ceiling lost in shadows, its walls lined with equipment that pulsed with lights in patterns she couldn't immediately parse.

And at its center, rising from the floor like a monument to everything wrong with Pale Cities philosophy, stood the Nullwave emitter array.

It was beautiful. That was the horror of it. The crystalline structures that formed its core were arranged in geometric patterns that seemed almost organic, almost like something the MNA might have grown. But they were not grown. They were manufactured, each crystal cut to precise specifications, each angle calculated to focus frequencies that the human mind was not meant to perceive.

The array was perhaps twenty meters tall, its spires reaching toward the ceiling like the fingers of a grasping hand. Cables ran from its base to monitoring stations arranged around the chamber's perimeter. And everywhere, everywhere, the lights pulsed in rhythms that made Aiyana's skin crawl, that reminded her of the moment the Nullwave had struck the border station, the moment Sitala had screamed in her mind.

She activated her recording device and began to document everything.

* * *

The monitoring stations told a story that was worse than she had imagined.

Aiyana moved from console to console, photographing screens, copying data to her portable storage device, absorbing information faster than she could process its implications. The Nullwave wasn't just a weapon. It was a network, exactly as Elias had said, distributed across Nova-Providence's power grid, with nodes at twelve separate locations throughout the city.

The test that had killed fourteen animals and wounded Sitala had used less than three percent of the system's total capacity.

At full power, the Nullwave could reach every Bioweb node within a thousand kilometers. Could silence every harmonic connection, every bonded animal, every organic system that the MNA had spent centuries building. A single coordinated pulse could cripple their entire civilization in minutes.

And according to the deployment schedule she found on one of the consoles, they were planning to do exactly that.

Operation Quiet Dawn. Launch date: seventeen days from now. Target: the MNA capital and all major population centers. Estimated impact: total disruption of Bioweb infrastructure, massive casualties among bonded animals, widespread system failures in food production, transportation, and communication.

The document didn't use the word genocide. But that was what it described. The systematic destruction of everything that made the MNA possible, dressed up in the clinical language of military operations.

Aiyana copied everything. Every file, every schematic, every piece of evidence that proved what the Pale Cities were planning. Her hands were trembling, but she forced them steady, forced herself to work methodically, to miss nothing.

She was so focused on her task that she almost missed the

sound of footsteps.

Almost.

She dropped behind a console bank just as a door on the far side of the chamber opened. Two technicians in gray uniforms emerged, their voices carrying across the vast space in the flat acoustics of underground architecture.

"...diagnostic's running clean so far. Another hour and we can sign off on the final calibration."

"Good. Director Chen wants everything perfect for the demonstration next week. Assembly observers are coming to see the facility."

"More politicians. Great. Just what we need."

The voices moved closer. Aiyana pressed herself against the console, making herself as small as possible, controlling her breathing. If they came around this bank, if they checked the station where she had been working...

The footsteps stopped. A console chirped nearby.

"Huh. Someone left a diagnostic running on Station Seven."

"Probably Reeves. He's always forgetting to log out."

"Should I...?"

"Leave it. We'll yell at him in the morning. Come on, I want to check the resonance chamber before Chen shows up."

The footsteps receded. A door opened and closed. Silence returned to the chamber, broken only by the eternal hum of the Nullwave array.

Aiyana allowed herself to breathe.

She had perhaps ten minutes before the diagnostic window closed and the motion sensors came back online. Ten minutes to finish her documentation and get out.

She moved quickly, photographing the final consoles, capturing the last pieces of evidence. Then she turned to leave.

And stopped.

There was another door on the far side of the chamber. Unmarked, unremarkable, easy to miss among the equipment arrays. But something about it drew her attention. Something about the way it sat slightly apart from the rest of the facility, as if what lay behind it wasn't quite part of the same operation.

She had the evidence she came for. She should leave now, while she still could.

But Kele might be somewhere in this city. Detained, Ford had said. Held for questioning. And if the Pale Cities were holding MNA prisoners, where better to keep them than in a facility that officially didn't exist?

She checked her time. Seven minutes. Just enough to look.

She crossed the chamber to the unmarked door and pressed Ford's card to the reader.

The light stayed red.

Access denied. Whatever was behind this door, Ford's credentials weren't enough to open it. Which meant it was classified beyond even his security level.

She photographed the door anyway, recorded its location, the markings on its frame, everything that might help identify what lay behind it. Then she tried the card again, hoping the first attempt had been a glitch.

The light pulsed red. Then again. And then a new light appeared on the reader's display, amber and blinking.

A soft tone sounded somewhere in the facility. Not loud. Not an alarm, exactly. More like a notification. A flag being raised.

Two failed access attempts on a restricted door, Aiyana realized, her stomach dropping. *The system logged it. Someone will check.*

She had just announced her presence to the entire security network.

From somewhere above, through layers of concrete and steel, she heard the distant sound of boots on metal. Moving fast.

She turned and ran for the exit, her footsteps echoing in the vast chamber, her heart pounding with the knowledge that she had just made a terrible mistake. The Nullwave array pulsed with light behind her, and somewhere in the facility, alerts were spreading, security teams were mobilizing, the window of escape was narrowing with every second.

She had the evidence. But getting out had just become much harder.

And it was her own fault.

* * *

She made it back to the junction chamber with seconds to spare, her lungs burning, her legs aching from the sprint up three flights of stairs.

Speaks-Low and Renna were waiting, their relief visible even in the dim light. But Aiyana's face told them something had gone wrong.

"What happened?" Speaks-Low demanded.

"I triggered a security flag. Tried to access a restricted door." The words came out between ragged breaths. "They'll be looking for the source. We need to move. Now."

Speaks-Low's expression flickered with something that might have been anger, might have been disappointment. But there was no time for recriminations. "Move," he ordered. "Extraction route. Fast."

They plunged back into the power conduits, moving faster now, driven by the knowledge that somewhere behind them, security teams were spreading out, searching for the intruder who had tripped their systems.

Kira was waiting at the relay point, her face tense. "I'm

picking up increased patrol activity on the surface. Something's making them nervous."

"That would be us," Aiyana said grimly. "I made a mistake. They know someone was in the facility."

Sitala's presence strengthened as they moved closer to the surface. The eagle was agitated, her thoughts carrying images of movement in the streets, of uniformed figures converging on locations throughout the city.

Many soldiers, Sitala thought. *Moving fast. Looking for someone.*

"Ford," Renna said quietly. "If they've connected the intrusion to his credentials..."

"Then we move faster." Speaks-Low's voice was iron. "Before they connect him to us."

They emerged from the conduits into the pre-dawn darkness of Nova-Providence. Somewhere in those streets, Captain Lucian Ford was about to be hunted because Aiyana had been reckless. Somewhere, the security alert she had triggered was spreading through the system, painting a target on everyone who had helped them.

Aiyana clutched the storage device against her chest. The evidence was worth everything. It had to be. Because the cost of obtaining it was already higher than she had imagined, and climbing with every passing moment.

She followed her team into the darkness, toward the extraction point, toward home.

And tried not to think about what her mistake might cost them before the night was over.

20

The Cost of Truth

They found Elias waiting at the extraction point, his face pale in the pre-dawn light.

The abandoned warehouse on Nova-Providence's eastern edge had been chosen for its proximity to the Frontier and its lack of surveillance coverage. Now, with patrols intensifying across the city, it felt less like a refuge and more like a trap waiting to close.

"Ford's been arrested," Elias said without preamble. His voice was steady, but Aiyana could see the tremor in his hands. "They came for him two hours ago. His apartment, his office, everywhere he might have gone. Someone reported suspicious activity on his access credentials."

"The installation," Speaks-Low said grimly. "They traced my entry to his card."

"Does he know about this location?" Renna was already scanning their surroundings, calculating escape routes.

"No. We kept the extraction details compartmentalized." Elias ran a hand through his hair. "But they'll interrogate him. Whatever he knows, they'll get it eventually. We don't have much time."

Aiyana thought of Ford in that basement, speaking of his daughter, his face haunted by what he had witnessed. He had known this might happen. Had made arrangements, he said. Had accepted the cost of his choice before he ever made it.

That didn't make it easier to bear.

"What about you?" she asked Elias. "If they're investigating Ford, they'll look at everyone he contacted. Your meeting at the dormitory..."

"I've already been questioned once." Elias's laugh was hollow. "Routine, they said. Just confirming my whereabouts during certain timeframes. I don't think they suspect me yet. But it's only a matter of time."

"Then come with us." The words were out before Aiyana could consider them. "Cross into MNA territory. You've done everything you can here."

Elias was quiet for a long moment. Through the warehouse's grimy windows, the first gray light of dawn was beginning to touch the sky. In an hour, maybe less, the city would wake fully, and their window for escape would narrow to nothing.

"My mother is still here," he said finally. "If I disappear, they'll go after her. Use her to draw me out, or punish her for my actions." He shook his head. "I can't leave her to face that alone."

"Elias..."

"I knew what I was doing when I started this." His voice firmed. "I knew there would be consequences. I just hoped I'd have more time to prepare for them." He reached into his jacket and pulled out a small data chip. "I found something else. Last night, after we talked. Information about detained MNA citizens."

Aiyana's heart lurched. "Kele?"

"I don't know. The records are fragmentary, heavily redacted. But there's a facility mentioned, somewhere in the northern sector. A place where 'subjects of interest' are held for extended questioning." He pressed the chip into her hand. "It's not much. But it's a start."

She closed her fingers around the chip, feeling its weight far beyond its physical size. Another piece of evidence. Another thread that might lead to her brother. Another debt she owed to a man who was choosing to stay behind and face whatever came.

"Thank you," she said. "For everything. I don't know how to..."

"Don't." Elias managed a small smile. "Don't thank me until it matters. Until what we've done makes a difference." He pulled out his father's compass and looked at it one last time. "My father died trying to find the truth. I think maybe he succeeded, and that's why they killed him. I'd rather live, if I can. But if I can't..." He shrugged. "At least I'll know I tried."

"We have to move," Speaks-Low said quietly. "Now, or not at all."

Elias nodded. "There's a drainage channel that runs under the eastern wall. Old infrastructure, mostly forgotten. It'll get you outside the city limits. From there, you know the way."

"Come with us," Aiyana said again, knowing he wouldn't, needing to say it anyway.

"I can't." He stepped back, putting distance between himself and the team. "But I can make sure you get out. I know some people who owe me favors. I can create a distraction, draw attention away from your route."

"That will expose you."

"Maybe. Maybe not." His smile turned rueful. "I've gotten good at not being noticed. Let me use that skill one more time."

There was nothing more to say. Aiyana reached out and gripped his hand, feeling the warmth of his fingers, the pulse of blood beneath skin. Two people from opposite sides of a war that had been building for centuries, connected by choices that neither of them could take back.

"Stay alive," she said. "Please."

"I'll try." He squeezed her hand once, then released it. "Now go. Before it's too late."

* * *

The drainage channel was everything Elias had promised: cramped, foul-smelling, and utterly unmonitored.

Aiyana crawled through the darkness with Sitala riding her shoulder, the eagle's wings folded tight against her body, her thoughts a constant stream of discomfort and determination. The bond between them pulsed with shared purpose: get through this, get home, make it matter.

Behind her, the team moved in single file. Renna first, then Kira, then Speaks-Low bringing up the rear. No one spoke. The only sounds were their breathing and the distant gurgle of water somewhere below.

They were halfway through when they heard the voices.

Echoing from behind them, distorted by the tunnel's acoustics but unmistakable: soldiers, calling to each other, the clatter of boots on metal. Someone had found the entrance. Someone was coming.

"Move," Speaks-Low hissed. "Faster."

They scrambled forward, abandoning stealth for speed. Aiyana's knees scraped against the channel floor, her palms slick with foul water, her lungs burning with the effort. Behind them, the voices grew louder. Closer. A flashlight beam cut through the darkness, sweeping the tunnel walls.

The alarm she had triggered. The extra time she had taken photographing that locked door. The patrols had been searching for them ever since, and now they had found the trail.

This is my fault, Aiyana realized. *I did this.*

A pale light appeared ahead. The exit. Fifty meters. Forty. Thirty.

Behind them, the soldiers were gaining. Aiyana could hear individual words now, commands shouted in clipped military cadence. They had weapons. They had numbers. They had every advantage except one.

"I'll hold them," Renna said.

"No." Aiyana twisted in the cramped space, trying to see her. "We all get out or none of us do."

"That's not your call." Renna's voice was calm, almost gentle. "The evidence has to reach the council. Nothing else matters. You know that."

"Renna..."

"Go." She was already turning, positioning herself to block the tunnel. "I'll buy you time. Get out. Get home. Make this mean something."

Speaks-Low's hand closed on Aiyana's arm, pulling her forward. "She's right. Move."

"I can't leave her. I can't..."

"You can. You will." His grip was iron. "Honor her choice by surviving it."

The last thing Aiyana saw before Speaks-Low dragged her toward the exit was Renna's face, lit by the approaching flashlights, set in an expression of absolute resolve. Then the tunnel curved and she was gone, and Aiyana was crawling toward the light with tears streaming down her face and Sitala's thoughts a desperate keening in her mind.

They emerged into gray morning light. Behind them, echoing up from the drainage channel, came the sounds of a struggle. Shouts. A cry of pain that might have been Renna's. Then silence.

"Run," Speaks-Low commanded. "Now. Don't look back."

Aiyana ran.

* * *

They moved through the Frontier in silence, three instead of four, the weight of Renna's absence pressing down on them like a physical thing.

Sitala flew ahead, scouting their path, but her thoughts were muted, colored by Aiyana's grief. The bond between them carried everything: the guilt, the rage, the desperate need to make Renna's sacrifice worth something.

Halfway to the MNA border, they stopped to rest in the shell of what had once been a community center. The walls still bore faded murals, images of people working together. A testament to integration that had failed.

"Report," Speaks-Low said, his voice businesslike despite the exhaustion in his eyes. "What did you find in there?"

Aiyana pulled out her storage device. "Everything. The Nullwave's full architecture. Its power requirements. Its range capabilities." She paused. "And their deployment plans. Operation Quiet Dawn. They're going to fire it at full power in seventeen days. Target: the MNA capital and all major population centers."

The silence that followed was absolute.

"At full power," Kira said slowly, "what would that mean?"

"Total disruption of the Bioweb within a thousand kilometers. Massive casualties among bonded animals. System failures across food production, transportation, communication." Aiyana's voice was flat, clinical. "They're not planning a demonstration. They're planning to destroy us."

"Then we have seventeen days to stop them." Speaks-Low's jaw was set. "We need to get this intelligence to the council immediately. Every hour counts."

"And Renna?" The words scraped out of Aiyana's throat. "What happens to her?"

Speaks-Low met her eyes. She saw the same grief there, the same guilt, carefully controlled. "She knew the risks. We all did. The mission came first."

"The mission came first because I made it necessary." Aiyana's voice cracked. "The alarm I triggered. The extra time I took. If I hadn't..."

"If you hadn't, we might not have the intelligence about detained citizens. About the facility where they're holding people like your brother." Speaks-Low's voice was hard but not unkind. "War is choices, Waketah. Every choice has costs. You don't get to choose which costs you pay."

It wasn't absolution. It wasn't meant to be. But it was the truth, and Aiyana held onto it like a lifeline as they rose and continued their march toward home.

* * *

They crossed back into MNA territory as the sun reached its zenith.

The silence of the Frontier gave way to the harmonic hum of the Bioweb, the constant background music of connection that Aiyana had grown up with. It washed over her like coming home, but the warmth couldn't touch the cold place that had formed in her chest.

Sitala screamed overhead, but her joy was tempered by Aiyana's grief. *Home*, the eagle thought. *But not whole. Not everyone.*

"We made it," Kira said quietly. It should have been Renna saying those words. It should have been four of them standing here, not three.

They pressed on toward Wakana Station. The evidence she carried could change everything. Could force the international community to intervene. Could expose the Pale Cities' plans and rally opposition before Operation Quiet Dawn could be launched.

Behind them, somewhere in Nova-Providence, Renna was in enemy hands. Ford was being interrogated. Elias was creating distractions, risking everything for people he had been taught to hate. And in a facility that officially didn't exist, MNA citizens were being held. Bridge-builders and idealists. People like Kele.

Aiyana clutched the data chip Elias had given her and kept walking. She would find her brother. Would bring Renna home. Would not rest until she had made this mean something.

She owed them that much. She owed everyone who had paid the price of her choices.

Above her, Sitala flew in widening circles, her golden feathers bright against the endless blue of the sky. The bond between them carried everything: grief and guilt and determination and the fierce refusal to let any of it be for nothing.

Aiyana lifted her face to the sun and kept walking toward home.

The Cold War had sixteen days left.

And she had debts to repay.

21

The Weight of Knowledge

The council chamber had never felt so small.

Chogan Grayfeather stood at the center of the speaking floor, the evidence from Operation Silent Measure projected onto screens that had been hastily installed around the room's perimeter. Fifty-three faces watched him in silence, their expressions ranging from horror to fury to something that looked almost like despair.

He had shown them everything. The Nullwave array in its crystalline glory. The network architecture that spread through Nova-Providence like a cancer. The deployment schedules, the targeting parameters, the clinical language of Operation Quiet Dawn that described the systematic destruction of their civilization as if it were nothing more than a logistics problem to be solved.

And now he waited for their response, knowing that whatever they decided would determine the fate of millions.

"Fifteen days," Speaker Wren Tallgrass said finally, her voice cutting through the silence like a blade. "They're planning to launch in fifteen days. And we're only learning about it now."

"We learned about it as soon as we could," Chogan replied evenly. "The operation to gather this intelligence was mounted within hours of the Nullwave test. Our team performed flawlessly under impossible conditions."

"And yet fifteen days may not be enough." Tallgrass rose from her seat, her eyes fixed on the screens. "What you're showing us is a weapon of genocide. A system designed to destroy everything we've built in a single coordinated strike. How do we stop something like that in fifteen days?"

"That is what this council must decide."

The chamber erupted into competing voices, representatives rising to offer opinions, strategies, fears. Chogan let them speak, knowing that they needed to process what they had seen before any rational discussion could occur. The evidence was overwhelming. The threat was existential. The options were all terrible in their own ways.

After several minutes, Elder Blackriver raised her hand for silence. The voices gradually subsided, drawn by the authority of her presence.

"We have three choices," she said, her voice carrying across the chamber. "We can strike first, attempt to destroy the Nullwave before it can be used against us. We can go public, share this evidence with the international community and hope that external pressure forces the Pale Cities to stand down. Or we can prepare our defenses and hope that we can survive whatever they throw at us."

"There's a fourth option," a voice called from the upper tiers. "We can negotiate. Use this evidence as leverage to force a genuine peace agreement."

"Negotiate?" Tallgrass's laugh was bitter. "With people who are planning to exterminate us? Who built a weapon specifically designed to kill our bonded companions and destroy our way of life?" She shook her head. "There is nothing to negotiate. There is only survival."

"And yet," Chogan said quietly, "our source inside the Pale Cities suggests that not everyone supports this plan. That there are factions within their government who want something other than war. Captain Ford, who provided us with access to the installation, is one such person. There may be others."

"One man. Perhaps a few sympathizers." Tallgrass waved dismissively. "Against the entire apparatus of a state that has spent decades building a weapon of genocide. Forgive me if I don't find that reassuring."

"It's not meant to be reassuring. It's meant to be accurate." Chogan met her eyes steadily. "We cannot pretend that the Pale Cities are a monolith. They have their own divisions, their own conflicts, their own people who question the path their leaders have chosen. Any strategy we adopt must account for that complexity."

* * *

The debate continued for hours, circling through the same arguments, the same fears, the same impossible choices.

A preemptive strike was rejected as too risky. They didn't know all the Nullwave nodes, couldn't guarantee they would destroy enough of the network to prevent retaliation. And the moment they attacked Pale Cities territory, they would be the aggressors, losing any moral high ground they currently held.

Pure defense was rejected as insufficient. The Nullwave's range was too great, its power too overwhelming. No amount of preparation could protect every population center, every food production facility, every critical node of their civilization.

That left international exposure. Sharing the evidence with

the world. Hoping that the pressure of global condemnation would force the Pale Cities to abandon their plans.

"It's a gamble," admitted Elder Nayeli, who had traveled from Wakana Station to present Commander Speaks-Low's operational report. "We cannot know how the international community will respond. Some nations may dismiss the evidence as fabricated. Others may decide that our conflict is not their concern. And even if they do respond, they may not respond quickly enough."

"But it gives us options," Blackriver said. "If we go public and the Pale Cities proceed anyway, we will have allies. Other nations who cannot ignore such blatant aggression. Trade partners who will impose costs. Voices that will speak for us in forums we cannot access alone."

"And if it doesn't work?" Tallgrass demanded. "If we expose everything and they launch Quiet Dawn anyway?"

"Then we will have done everything we could." Chogan's voice was heavy. "And whatever survives will have the truth. Will know what was done to us and by whom. Will carry that knowledge forward, whatever form the future takes."

The silence that followed was different from the silences that had come before. This was the silence of people confronting the possibility of their own extinction. Of understanding that some threats could not be fully countered, only faced.

"There is one more thing," Chogan said. He gestured, and a new image appeared on the screens. A map of Nova-Providence, with a location in the northern sector highlighted. "Our team discovered evidence that the Pale Cities are holding MNA citizens. Bridge-builders and others who were captured in the Frontier. We don't know how many or in what conditions, but we know they exist."

Murmurs rippled through the chamber. Missing persons had been a persistent concern for years, families who had lost contact with loved ones who ventured into the gray lands. Now they had confirmation that at least some of those people had not simply vanished.

"If we go public," Chogan continued, "we demand their release. Make it part of our case to the international community. The Pale Cities are not just planning genocide. They are already holding our people prisoner, in violation of every principle of civilized behavior."

"And if they respond by killing the prisoners?" The question came from somewhere in the upper tiers, voiced quietly but heard by everyone.

"That is a risk we cannot eliminate." Chogan's voice was steady, though Aiyana, watching from the observers' gallery, could see the cost of that steadiness in the set of his shoulders. "But staying silent to protect them condemns millions of others. We cannot make that trade. We cannot let the threat to a few paralyze our response to a threat against all."

Aiyana thought of Kele, somewhere in that city of steel and silence. Thought of the data chip in her pocket, the fragmentary evidence of where he might be held. Going public might save their civilization. It might also seal her brother's fate.

She understood, in that moment, why Chogan had looked so old when he sent her on this mission. Why every decision he made seemed to cost him something he could never get back. This was what leadership meant. Choosing which sacrifices to make. Living with the consequences of choices that had no good options.

* * *

The vote came as the sun began to set, casting long shadows

through the woven dome above.

Forty-one in favor of international exposure. Twelve opposed, arguing that the risks were too great, that they should seek other options first. The motion passed, but the margin was closer than Chogan had hoped. The council was not united. Could not be, in the face of such terrible choices.

"The decision is made," Elder Blackriver announced formally. "We will share the evidence gathered by Operation Silent Measure with the international community. We will demand that the Pale Cities dismantle the Nullwave network and release all detained MNA citizens. And we will make clear that any attack on our territory will be met with the full response our alliance can muster."

"What about our defenses?" Tallgrass asked. "Even if the international response is favorable, we cannot assume the Pale Cities will comply."

"Defensive preparations will continue in parallel," Chogan said. "Every Bioweb node that can be hardened will be hardened. Every bonded animal that can be protected will be protected. We will not assume that exposure alone will save us." He paused. "But we will give peace every chance to succeed before we accept that war is inevitable."

The session ended with assignments, responsibilities, deadlines. Communications teams to prepare the evidence for international distribution. Diplomatic teams to reach out to potential allies. Defense teams to accelerate protective measures. Everyone had a role. Everyone had work to do.

As the representatives filed out of the chamber, Chogan remained on the speaking floor, his head bowed, his shoulders carrying the weight of everything that had been decided.

Aiyana descended from the observers' gallery and approached him. She had not spoken during the session, had not been invited to speak, but she could not leave without saying something.

"Elder Grayfeather."

He looked up, and for a moment she saw something in his eyes that she had never seen before. Not defeat, exactly. Something closer to exhaustion. The weariness of someone who had been fighting the same battle for thirty years and still didn't know if he was winning or losing.

"Engineer Waketah." His voice softened slightly. "You did well. The intelligence you gathered may have saved us. May save us still, if the world responds the way we hope."

"I had help. Elias. Ford. People inside the Pale Cities who risked everything because they believed there had to be another way."

"Yes." Chogan nodded slowly. "That may be the most important thing you brought back. The proof that not everyone on the other side wants this war. That there are people over there who are as horrified by what their government is doing as we are." He paused. "In the end, that may matter more than any weapon. The knowledge that we have potential allies, even in enemy territory."

"What happens now?"

"Now we wait. We prepare. We hope." He managed a tired smile. "The same things we've been doing for decades. The same things we'll keep doing until either peace comes or war forces us to stop."

"And Kele? The other prisoners?"

"We demand their release as part of our international appeal. We make clear that their continued detention is part of the case against the Pale Cities." Chogan's voice was gentle but honest.

"Whether that helps them or hurts them, I cannot say. But silence would certainly not help them. And it would not help the millions who depend on us to do everything in our power to prevent this war."

Aiyana nodded, accepting the answer she had known she would receive. There were no good options. Only choices between different kinds of terrible.

"Thank you," she said. "For trusting me with this mission. For believing I could do it."

"Thank yourself," Chogan replied. "You earned that trust. And you'll have opportunities to earn it again, in the days ahead." His eyes held hers. "This isn't over, Aiyana. Whatever happens in the next fifteen days, whatever the world decides, there will be more work to do. More risks to take. More impossible choices to make."

"I know." She straightened her shoulders. "I'll be ready."

She left him standing alone in the chamber, surrounded by screens that showed evidence of genocide and the faces of people who had risked everything to gather it. Behind her, the sun finished setting, plunging the room into the soft glow of bioluminescent lighting.

Fifteen days.

In fifteen days, the Pale Cities would either back down or launch their attack. In fifteen days, the Cold War would either end or transform into something far worse. In fifteen days, everything would change.

Aiyana stepped out into the evening air, where Sitala was waiting on a perch near the chamber's entrance. The eagle's golden feathers caught the last light of day, glowing like fire against the darkening sky.

What now? Sitala asked through the bond.

Now we wait, Aiyana replied. *We prepare. We hope. And we stay ready for whatever comes next.*

Together?

Always together.

The eagle launched from her perch and circled overhead, a silhouette against the emerging stars. Aiyana watched her fly, feeling the bond between them pulse with everything they had survived and everything they still had to face.

The evidence was gathered. The council had decided. The world would soon know what the Pale Cities were planning.

Now came the hardest part: waiting to see if truth was enough to prevent a war.

22

The Harmonic Divide

The world learned the truth on the fourteenth day. But truth, Aiyana was learning, came with a price.

She watched the broadcasts from a monitoring station near the eastern border, the same station where she had felt Sitala nearly die in her arms. The screens showed feeds from international networks, their anchors struggling to contextualize evidence that defied easy explanation. Images of the Nullwave array. Schematics of the network spreading through Nova-Providence's power grid. Documents detailing Operation Quiet Dawn.

And testimony from Commander Speaks-Low, recorded before the council, describing how they had gathered this evidence. How they had infiltrated the facility. How they had lost Renna during the extraction.

Renna. Aiyana closed her eyes, remembering the moment everything had gone wrong. The alarm that shouldn't have triggered. The patrol that appeared from a corridor Ford's intelligence hadn't mapped. Aiyana had wanted to go back for her. Had argued, had pulled against Speaks-Low's grip until he'd physically dragged her toward the extraction point.

"She knew the risks," he'd said afterward, his voice flat with the discipline of a man who had lost people before. *"We all did. The mission came first."*

But Aiyana knew the truth he wouldn't say: the alarm had triggered because of her. Because she'd pushed too far into the facility, trying to photograph that locked door, the one that might have held prisoners like Kele. She'd been reckless. And Renna had paid the price.

The international reaction was immediate and fractured.

Some nations condemned the Pale Cities, demanding immediate dismantlement of the weapon. Others questioned the evidence's authenticity, suggesting it might be fabricated to justify MNA expansion. Three eastern powers issued a joint statement supporting Nova-Providence's "right to defensive technology," calling the MNA's infiltration "an act of war that cannot go unanswered."

The coalition Chogan had hoped for was not forming. It was splintering before it could begin.

* * *

The message arrived at midnight, routed through channels that grew more dangerous with each use.

Aiyana opened it with trembling fingers.

Ford executed yesterday. Public announcement tomorrow. They're calling him a traitor who acted alone. Using his death to deny everything.

The words hit her like a physical blow. Ford was dead. The man who had given them everything, who had sacrificed his career and his life for people he had been taught to hate.

His daughter got out. The network took her before the arrest. He made sure of that first.

Small comfort. But comfort nonetheless.

Drax is triumphant. The evidence hasn't weakened her. It's made her stronger. She's using it to prove that the MNA is the aggressor, that we sent spies into their territory, violated their sovereignty. Half the Assembly believes her. The other half is too afraid to disagree.

They've captured one of your team. A woman named Renna. She's being held at a facility in the northern sector. They're calling her a terrorist.

Aiyana's stomach turned to ice. Renna was alive. Alive and in their hands because Aiyana had been reckless, because she'd thought finding Kele was worth any risk.

The Nullwave array wasn't damaged. Our evidence only showed what it is, not where all of it is. They're already building redundant nodes. By next month, there will be three arrays instead of one. Exposure didn't stop them. It accelerated them.

She read the final lines, her heart pounding.

Halding is proposing a summit. Don't trust it. It's not an olive branch. It's a delay while they finish construction. By the time negotiations conclude, they'll have the capability to silence your entire network in a single strike.

I don't know how much longer I can stay hidden. They're looking for the leak. Looking for me. When they find me, and they will, I won't be able to warn you again.

Whatever happens, I don't regret it. Any of it. But I need you to understand: this isn't over. It's just beginning.

There was no signature. There didn't need to be.

* * *

The sun rose on the fifteenth day, and Prime Councillor Rowan Halding appeared on screens across the world.

His face was composed, almost serene. The face of a man

who had already won and was simply managing the aftermath.

"The Pale Cities categorically reject the allegations made against us. The evidence presented by the Many Nations Alliance is a fabrication, designed to justify their illegal incursion into our sovereign territory and their murder of loyal citizens who died defending our borders."

Aiyana watched the broadcast from the monitoring station, her hands clenched at her sides. Murder. They were calling Ford's execution murder by the MNA. Were claiming the team had killed guards during the infiltration. Were rewriting history in real time.

"However," Halding continued, "in the interest of peace and in recognition of international concern, we are prepared to enter negotiations regarding verification of our defensive capabilities. We propose a summit on neutral ground, where all parties can present their evidence and discuss a path toward mutual security."

It was not an admission. It was not a retreat. It was exactly what Elias had warned: a delay. A performance of reasonableness while the Quiet Choir built their redundant arrays, while Drax consolidated power, while the world's attention drifted to other crises.

The Cold War had not ended. It had simply learned to wear a different mask.

* * *

Three days later, Aiyana stood at her mother's door.

Takoda opened it before she could knock, her face showing the strain of weeks of uncertainty. They embraced in the doorway, but the warmth couldn't touch the cold place that had formed in Aiyana's chest.

"You're home," Takoda said. "You're really home."

"I'm home." But even as she said it, Aiyana knew it wasn't entirely true. Part of her was still in Nova-Providence, in that corridor where she'd pushed too far, in the moment when Renna had told her to run and she had.

Inside, over tea neither of them drank, she told her mother what she could. Not everything. Not the recklessness, not the guilt, not the way she woke each night hearing phantom alarms. But enough.

"The summit they're proposing," Takoda said. "Do you think it will accomplish anything?"

"No." The word came out harder than Aiyana intended. "It's a trap. A way to look reasonable while they prepare for war. By the time negotiations fail, and they will fail, the Nullwave network will be unstoppable."

"Then what was the point?" Takoda's voice cracked. "What was any of it for, if nothing changed?"

Aiyana stared at her untouched tea. "I don't know. We exposed the truth. We proved what they were building. And it didn't matter. They just... absorbed it. Turned it into another weapon."

"And Kele?"

The question she had been dreading. Aiyana pulled the data chip from her pocket, the one that had cost Renna her freedom. "There's a facility in the northern sector. They hold MNA citizens there. Bridge-builders. People like Kele." She paused. "And now they're holding Renna there too. Because of me."

"Because of you?"

"I pushed too far. Tried to find information about Kele when I should have been focused on the mission. An alarm triggered. Renna stayed behind so the rest of us could escape." The words tasted like ash. "I traded her for the possibility of finding him.

And I didn't even succeed."

Takoda was quiet for a long moment. When she spoke, her voice was gentle but unflinching. "Your brother made a choice to cross into dangerous territory because he believed it was right. You made a choice too. The difference is, you have to live with the consequences of yours."

"How do I do that?"

"By making sure it means something. By not letting Renna's sacrifice, or Ford's, or any of it, be for nothing." Takoda reached across the table and took her daughter's hand. "The truth is out there now. It may not have stopped them, but it changed things. Changed what people know, what they're willing to believe. That matters. Even if we can't see how yet."

* * *

That night, alone on the observation deck where she had once watched her brother walk away, Aiyana received one final message.

Not from Elias. The routing was different, the encryption unfamiliar. She almost deleted it unread.

But something made her open it.

You exposed one array. We have built three more. You saved evidence. We have buried witnesses. You think you won a battle. You have only shown us where to strike next.

The summit will proceed. Your diplomats will negotiate in good faith. Ours will not. When the talks collapse, and they will collapse, the world will blame your intransigence. Your aggression. Your refusal to accept peace.

We are patient. We have been patient for centuries. We can wait a little longer.

But not forever.

Remember what silence sounds like. You will hear it again soon.

The message deleted itself before she could respond. Before she could trace it. Before she could do anything but stand in the darkness, her heart pounding, the Quiet Choir's promise echoing in her mind.

Sitala landed on the railing beside her, feathers ruffled by the night wind. Through the bond, Aiyana felt the eagle's fierce presence, her refusal to surrender to fear.

They threaten, Sitala observed. *We endure.*

"Is that enough?" Aiyana whispered. "Just enduring?"

It is what we have. Today. Now. The eagle's thoughts carried no comfort, only truth. *Tomorrow, we fight for more.*

Aiyana looked east, toward the Frontier, toward the gray lands where her brother had disappeared, where Renna was now imprisoned, where the Quiet Choir was building weapons that could silence everything she loved.

The Cold War had not ended. Had not even paused. It had simply shown its true face: patient, implacable, willing to play a longer game than anyone on her side had imagined.

She thought of Kele's last words to her, spoken in anger and love: *Someone has to prove that the gap can be crossed.*

He had tried. Ford had tried. Elias was still trying, somewhere in Nova-Providence, hunted and alone. And Renna, captured because of Aiyana's recklessness, was paying the price for all of them.

The gap remained. Wider now, perhaps, than it had ever been.

But Aiyana would not stop trying to cross it. Would not abandon Renna to the silence. Would not let Ford's sacrifice, or Kele's faith, or Elias's courage mean nothing.

She would find another way. Even if it cost her everything.

Even if she had to become the bridge herself.

Above her, the stars wheeled in their ancient patterns, indifferent to the wars of the world below. The Bioweb hummed with tension she could feel in her bones. And somewhere in the darkness, the Quiet Choir waited, patient as stone, certain as death.

The harmonic divide remained.

But tomorrow, she would begin again.

23

Three Weeks Later

The safe house was a storage room behind a recycling facility in Nova-Providence's industrial sector, where the air tasted of rust and the Signal Mesh broadcasts couldn't penetrate the layers of metal shielding.

Elias had been here for nine days. He had stopped counting the hours.

The network that had helped Ford's daughter escape had taken him in after the purges began. Junior staff from the Cultural Ministry, archivists who had asked too many questions, anyone connected to the summit delegation who wasn't already under Drax's protection. Most had been arrested. Some had simply vanished. Elias had been lucky, if hiding in a metal box while his face appeared on security bulletins could be called luck.

He passed the time reading. The network had access to materials that would have earned him execution if found in his possession: uncensored histories, MNA publications, accounts of the Long March that bore no resemblance to what he had learned in school. Each document peeled back another layer of the lies he had been raised on. Each revelation made returning to his old life more impossible.

Not that returning was an option anymore.

The message came through the network's encrypted channel at dawn on the tenth day. He almost missed it; he had been sleeping, or trying to, curled on a pallet of insulation material that smelled of chemicals and old metal.

Three words. No signature. No return address.

We're coming for her.

Elias read it twice. Three times. Felt something loosen in his chest that he hadn't known was clenched.

Renna. They were coming for Renna.

He didn't know how. Didn't know when. Didn't know if the message was even meant for him, or if he had intercepted something intended for other eyes. But it meant the MNA hadn't given up. Meant that somewhere beyond the gray borders of his dying city, people were still fighting.

He pulled his father's compass from his pocket. The needle still pointed east, toward everything he had lost. But east wasn't the only direction anymore.

He began composing a reply. Carefully. Precisely. Everything he knew about the northern detention facility, the patrol schedules he had memorized from classified briefings, the access codes that might still work if they hadn't been changed.

It wasn't much. But it was what he had.

And if they were coming, he intended to help them succeed.

* * *

The briefing room at Wakana Station had been converted into a war council.

Aiyana stood at the edge of the gathering, Sitala perched on the stand beside her, watching as Commander Speaks-Low laid out the intelligence on the central display. Satellite imagery of the northern detention complex. Guard rotation patterns. Entry points. Vulnerabilities.

Three weeks of planning. Three weeks of gathering resources, calling in favors, negotiating with factions who thought the mission was suicide and factions who thought it wasn't aggressive enough. Three weeks of Aiyana waking each night with Renna's face behind her eyes, with the weight of a debt she could never fully repay.

"The summit negotiations begin in six days," Speaks-Low said, his voice carrying the flat calm of a man who had accepted what was coming. "The Pale Cities delegation will expect us to be focused on diplomacy. They will not expect a secondary operation."

"They'll be watching the border," Elder Blackriver countered. "Security will be heightened precisely because of the summit."

"They'll be watching the wrong places." Speaks-Low tapped the display, highlighting a route that wound through terrain Aiyana recognized from her first mission. "We have new intelligence. From inside."

Elias. It had to be. Still alive, still fighting, still finding ways to reach across the divide.

"The objective is extraction," Speaks-Low continued. "Renna and any other MNA citizens held at the facility. Secondary objective: intelligence on the Nullwave expansion. Tertiary: any information regarding detained bridge-builders."

Kele. He didn't say the name, but Aiyana heard it anyway.

"This is not a military operation," Chogan Grayfeather said quietly from his seat near the back. He looked older than he had at the summit, the weight of failed diplomacy visible in every line of his face. "We cannot afford to give the Quiet Choir the war they want. If this mission is detected, if it escalates, everything we've worked for collapses."

"We know the risks," Speaks-Low replied. "We accept them."

His eyes found Aiyana across the room. She felt the question in his gaze, the weight of what he was asking. Last time, her recklessness had cost them Renna. Last time, she had let her personal mission override the team's safety.

This time would be different. It had to be.

"I'm ready," she said. The words came out steadier than she felt. "Whatever it takes."

Speaks-Low nodded once. "Then we begin preparations tonight. We move in four days."

The briefing continued, but Aiyana's mind had already traveled ahead, across the Frontier, into the gray heart of enemy territory. Renna was waiting. Kele might be waiting. And somewhere in Nova-Providence, hidden in the cracks of a crumbling empire, Elias was waiting too.

The harmonic divide remained. But they were learning to cross it, one impossible mission at a time.

Sitala stirred beside her, golden feathers catching the light.

Ready? the eagle asked.

Aiyana rested her hand on Sitala's back, feeling the steady pulse of her heartbeat, the bond that had carried them through everything and would carry them through whatever came next.

Ready, she replied.

Outside the window, the sun was setting over the mountains, painting the sky in shades of amber and rose. Somewhere beyond that horizon, the Pale Cities waited. The Quiet Choir waited. A war that had been building for centuries waited to finally consume them all.

But not today.

Today, there was still time.

And Aiyana intended to use every moment of it.

THE STORY CONTINUES IN

BOOK TWO: THE QUIET BORDER

Author's Note

This novel imagines a world that never was: a North America where Indigenous nations formed a continental alliance, where colonial settlement unfolded under Indigenous authority, and where two radically different societies now face each other across an ideological divide. It is speculative fiction, rooted in a simple question: What if history had bent differently?

The Many Nations Alliance depicted in these pages is a fictional composite. It draws inspiration from the philosophies, governance structures, and ecological relationships of numerous Indigenous cultures across North America, but it does not represent any single nation, tribe, or tradition. The technologies, rituals, and social structures of the MNA are inventions of this story, extrapolated from real principles of reciprocity, balance, and environmental stewardship that many Indigenous cultures share, but shaped into something new for the purposes of this narrative.

I want to be clear about what this book is and is not. It is not an attempt to speak for Indigenous peoples or to represent their lived experiences. It is not a claim to cultural knowledge I do not possess. It is, instead, an act of imagination that takes seriously the idea that other ways of organizing society, technology, and humanity's relationship with the natural world are not only possible but have always existed alongside the path Western civilization chose to follow.

The animal bonds portrayed in this story are meant as relationships, not magic. They require work, mutual respect, and ongoing consent from both partners. No character is born with an innate right to such a bond; they are earned through patience and attunement. I have tried to ensure that these relationships never imply genetic superiority, spiritual entitlement, or abilities unavailable to others through different paths. If I have fallen short of this intention anywhere, the failure is mine alone.

The Pale Cities, too, are a fictional creation. They are not meant as a direct allegory for any particular nation or political movement, though readers may find resonances with various historical and contemporary societies. The people who live within them are not villains by nature; they are people shaped by the stories their culture tells, struggling to survive within systems they did not build and may not fully understand. The conflict at the heart of this series is ideological, not ethnic. It is a collision between ways of seeing the world, not between peoples who are inherently good or evil.

I am grateful to the scholars, writers, and knowledge keepers whose work has shaped my understanding of Indigenous history, philosophy, and resistance. Any wisdom in these pages is borrowed; any errors are my own. I have tried to approach this material with humility, curiosity, and respect, knowing that imagination is not the same as knowledge, and that fiction, however well-intentioned, cannot substitute for the voices of those whose ancestors actually lived these alternatives.

This story asks what might have been. It does not presume to say what should be, or to speak for those who continue to carry forward the traditions, languages, and wisdom that colonialism tried to erase. If this novel inspires readers to seek out those voices directly, to learn from Indigenous writers, historians, and communities in their own words, then it will have accomplished something worthwhile beyond entertainment.

Thank you for reading.